Across State Lines

Lauren Biel

This is a work of fiction. Names, characters, events, and incidents are the products of the author's imagination. Any resemblance to actual persons, living or dead, or actual events is purely coincidental.

Library of Congress Cataloging-in-Publication Data

Across State Lines/Lauren Biel 1st ed.

Cover Design: Pretty in Ink

Content Editing: Sugar Free Editing

Interior Design: Sugar Free Editing

For more information on this book and the author, visit: www.LaurenBiel.com

Please visit LaurenBiel.com for a full list of content warnings.

*This is for the readers who know they shouldn't take a ride from strangers but hop right in when he has a pierced or tattooed d*ck*

Chapter One

Kane

The thick scent of diesel smoke fills the air as a herd of eighteen-wheelers idles in the truck stop's side lot. Some of the truckers have already bedded down for the night, tucked away in the small compartments in the backs of their cabs. Others—like me—still sit behind the wheel. Watching. Contemplating.

Decrepit lot lizards stroll by, their faces caked with makeup to cover the wrinkles of age or the scabs from drug use. They seem to know only one hairstyle tonight: stringy and greasy. They scuttle from truck to truck, more like insects than lizards. Parasites.

I draw a cigarette from my front pocket and light it. None of these women look interesting enough to pick up, so I lean back and inhale a cloud of cigarette smoke rather than spent diesel fuel. My body begins to relax as the nicotine finds a path to my mind, and I flick the ash out the cracked window. I wouldn't want to dirty my house, and for long-haul truckers like me, that's exactly what my cab is. My home.

"Hey, daddy!" a blonde catcalls from across the lot. She waggles her stubby fingers at me, trying to catch my attention.

I turn my head as if she's not there. I'm not interested. If I see someone I want, she won't need to beg for my attention. It's like a rig this size crashing into me when I see the right woman.

If it seems like I'm being picky, it's because I am. I like a very specific type of woman. Someone who still shines through the filth. Someone who isn't too far gone, unlike all the women skulking through the lot tonight. It's too late for them. The grime sinks to their bones, tainting them.

"You looking for some fun?" the blonde says as she reaches my window and scratches her cheek until blood rises to the surface.

I raise the window, stifling her voice. Cigarette smoke fills my cab, but that's better than having to listen to the lot lizard's attempts at begging. She gets the hint and wanders to the next truck, her metaphorical cup still held outward.

Settling back in my seat, my eyes catch on a raven-haired woman standing on her own. She lacks the brazen confidence the experienced women possess. As she clutches her elbows and peers through a sea of metal and asphalt, she looks so out of place.

I look twice, just to make sure she isn't an apparition born from my desperation. When I'm certain she's real, I roll down my window, lean out, and whistle toward her with a wave of my hand. Greedy, drug-hazed eyes turn toward me from all directions, but I'm only focused on her. I whistle again, struggling to be heard over the rumble of engines, but this time she turns her dark eyes toward me.

She points to her chest, asking a silent question. I nod, and she shuffles toward my truck.

"You need a ride?" I ask when she reaches my window.

Her eyes run the length of my truck before landing on me once more. She licks her lips and says, "Yeah, I do."

We don't discuss the logistics of where she needs to go because she doesn't actually want to go anywhere. She wants me to let her into the back of my cab, fuck her, hand her some money, and let her out again. She'll wait around and do it over and over to make her quota for the night.

"Hop in," I say, a forced smile on my face. I'm naturally gruff and intimidating, with tattoos all over my body and a tall frame packed with muscle. If I don't force a smile, even the most desperate lizard will run off.

She opens the passenger door and climbs inside. My riding companion, a brown mutt I call Pup, barks at her. Pup doesn't like anyone, which is probably why we get along so well. We make an odd couple—a big, burly trucker with a small, furry dog—but she's the only other living being I can trust.

"Quiet down," I say to the dog, and her barks shift to an agitated whine.

I stand up and head toward the back, knowing the girl will follow me. She has one thing on her mind, after all.

And so do I.

Pup tries to follow as well, but she'll only get in the way.

"Stay," I command, and she settles in the seat again.

I motion toward the bed in the rear of the cab, and the woman steps past me. Beneath the filth on her face, I can see glimpses of how pretty she could have been, but then my eyes focus on her neck. Her heartbeat pulses beneath the thin flesh, and I can't look away from it. The whore takes my steadfast gaze as a sign of unbridled attraction, so she leans into me and ghosts her fingertips over my chest.

"What do you want?" she asks.

She wants to know what I want her to do to me, whether I want her to suck my dick or let me put my cock inside her worn-out cunt. I don't want her to do anything to me. I couldn't do anything, even if she tried her best. Physically, I'm broken in that way. Realistically, I'm broken in too many ways.

I gently grip her hands and ease them away from my chest.

"Oh, come on, baby," she says. "You didn't let me into your truck to talk about the weather. What do you want me to do to you?"

"Nothing."

This woman would harden any other man's cock—she's fuckable, even if she's a lot whore—but mine remains limp.

Her hands move toward me again, going lower this time, and I nearly jump out of my skin at the brush of her touch. As she strokes me through my jeans, my ears start ringing. Panic tries to overtake my senses, and I force back the feeling by staring at that rapid flutter of her pulse in her neck.

"You're fucking limp, dude," she says, her voice rising to an annoyed pitch. "What? I don't get you hard?"

She almost sounds offended, and I don't blame her. Women like her measure their worth by how quickly they can get a man to come, and she can't even get me hard. But it isn't her fault. Not really.

She applies more pressure, desperate to prove she can do her job. I rip her hand away. She screams from the pressure I apply as I twist her wrist, but no one can hear anything outside this truck.

"Let go of me, you fucking *freak*!" she screams.

My fingers move to her neck, covering that beating pulse, and I squeeze until it feels as if it's inside me. Her hands fly to my wrists, clawing as she tries to free herself, but she's not strong enough. They never are.

I lift her onto the tips of her toes and squeeze harder. Her shoes scrabble beneath her, and she lands a weak kick against my shin. If she'd tried that when she still had enough oxygen in her brain, it might have stung a little, but she doesn't have the power to do any harm now.

The drumbeat beneath my fingers grows fainter before turning erratic. Then it finally stops. I continue to hold her in place as her eyes fixate forward, looking directly into mine.

Taking her life makes my lifeless heart beat faster. It warms the cold spaces hidden away in the dark crevices of my fractured soul. It's much more fulfilling to kill her than it would be to spend ten minutes fucking her, and best of all, it doesn't cost me a thing—aside from the price of a ticket to hell, but I've had a seat on that black train for a while now.

I drop the whore to the floor and lean back against the galley wall with quick, pleasure-filled breaths. Pup hops down from her seat and ventures over to sniff the dead woman's feet before sitting on her haunches and looking up at me as if she's glad the intruder is dead. I reach down and pet her.

Pup is a fascinating creature because as much as I like to watch the life leave the eyes of living things, I couldn't do that to her. When I found her on the side of the road a couple of years ago, broken and bleeding after being hit by a car, I went against every fiber of my being and saved her instead of ending her. I took her to the vet, and the rest is history. She's a three-legged spitfire with a gnarly little attitude, but she's mine, and she doesn't judge me for all the terrible things I do.

"Come on, Pup," I say as I head toward the front again. "Our night isn't over yet."

I can't exactly keep a dead body in the truck, so we'll need to find a good spot to dispose of the trash. And even though this one isn't cold yet, I'm already thinking about the next time. The high only lasts a few days, and then I'll need another fix. When I'm miles away, I'll pull into another lot like this one so I can repeat the process.

Hopefully it lasts a little longer next time. I prefer to play with my victims before releasing them into the black void, but this whore pushed a button when she called me a freak.

Freak. Psycho. Weirdo.

I've heard it all my life. Anyone who's around me long enough to form an opinion usually comes to the same conclusion. Something isn't right with Kane Hargrave. And even though I don't like when they point it out, they're not wrong.

I start up the truck and pull out of the lot. No one will notice that she's gone missing. New girls like her haven't been around long enough to get dirty yet, but they also haven't been around long enough to become accepted into the old hands' inner circle. She might have a pimp to report to, but he'll just assume she ran off with a trucker. It happens.

A few miles outside of town, I find a wooded area with a dirt service road. It's perfect. I'm not hauling any freight at the moment, so it's easy enough to find a lonely stretch of road with a space big enough to pull my rig to the side without jostling the contents. I can't exactly hide the massive thing, but I'm careful about where I stop.

Pup hops down from the truck as I gather the shovel and the body. After walking into the woods and finding a spot that isn't cluttered with tree roots—they're too hard to punch through, even for a guy my size—I set to work.

"One, two, there's been a few. Three, four, bury the whore," I sing as I dig. The soft soil spreads around the shovel's blade before I pull it up and toss the clump of earth to the side. Darkness shrouds me, hiding me beneath its protective cloak.

As I continue digging, I glance at the woman's lifeless eyes staring into a starry sky. They were such pretty eyes. Too bad they belonged to someone stupid enough to get into my truck.

I take a moment to rest when I'm halfway finished with the digging. Burying these girls is a lot harder than it used to be. I have to go pretty deep to avoid getting caught, but at forty years old, I'm not as young as I used to be. By now I should be married with kids or something so I can pass on all my fucked-up genes. Instead, I'm a prolific serial killer working along the I-90.

Being a long-haul trucker makes it too easy for a guy like me to find and dispose of women, leaving bodies along the interstate like breadcrumbs. No one ever traces it back to me, though. I had a scare once. A pack of coyotes managed to dig up what I'd planted beneath the soil, and they dragged it close enough to the road to catch some attention. That's why I bury them deeper now.

A headache buzzes behind my eyes as I drive the shovel into the ground again. I take a deep breath, trying to stay in control. Those fuckers aren't like me. They aren't damaged and deranged, even though the damage I've endured has forced them into being. They'll try to "help," but that's like sending out a medical resident to perform fucking brain surgery. They aren't cut out for this.

Worst of all, they always try to stop me, and I refuse to be stopped when I'm itching for a kill. Whether I get a chain around her neck or, like tonight, I use my bare hands, I need to feel the girl fight and buck for dear life beneath me. I need to feel her nails clawing at me with the desperation that is so typical of the dying. And like I said, no one ever misses them. They were lost and forgotten girls before I got my hands on them.

But it isn't right to call them forgotten. I never forget them, and maybe that's some consolation for their pathetic lives. The kills live in my mind forever. When I lie on my deathbed, my life won't flash before my eyes, but their deaths will.

I toss her body into the hole and begin shoving the soil over her. I start at the feet, saving the face for last. It's the eyes. I want to see them for as long as possible. When I finally cover them, it's over. Finished.

Until next time.

Once I've patted down the earth and moved some leaf litter, twigs, and a rotting log on top of the grave, I turn and look at my truck. Such a beauty. I call her The Purple Wet Dream. She's stacked. Chrome-plated everything, with a chameleon-painted tractor unit. Its color shifts with the light, oscillating between deeper and brighter shades of purple. I never thought someone like me could afford a machine like her, but I pulled some . . . side jobs . . . to afford her. She's literally what wet dreams are made of for guys like us.

I spent a metric fuck ton of money so I would have a ride that looked better than the ramshackle house I used to own. This truck is my true home, where I eat, sleep, and kill.

I want to do all those things in a beautiful place, and she's beautiful. And automatic, which leaves my hands free for other activities. Eating . . . torturing . . . You know, the usual.

This dead girl was beautiful too. What can I say? I like pretty things. Even when they're wrapped in shit, I can see the beauty beneath the initial layer of grime. Those are my kinds of women—tarnished but waiting to be polished to a shine. And once she's nice and shiny, I dirty her all over again.

Well, that's what I usually do. I enjoy cleaning them up and making them look nice before I end them, but I was overtaken by anger with this one and kind of skipped that step. Some might say I spend too much time on these bitches when I just plan to kill them in the end, but I can't keep them. They hate me. They'd run off the moment they could, and that isn't an option. You don't stay out of prison and avoid getting caught by letting them live. They all gotta die.

Whining at my feet draws my attention. Pup's tail thumps against my legs. Her half-curled ears flick back and forth as she listens to the scurry of a nocturnal creature in the bushes. We're far enough away from the road that we can hear the sounds of nature instead of tires humming on asphalt. The muscles beneath her fur tense, and I grab her collar to stop her from going after the fading sounds scuffling through the leaves. I don't want her running off. She's the only thing in my life that has remained consistent.

"Let's get back in the truck, Pup."

Now that I'm done burying that girl, I let the hum in my head intensify. I squint my eyes against the growing buzz in my brain. If he wants to come out now, he can. He can provide a break from my evil thoughts. My ailing mind.

After all, isn't that what I created him for?

Chapter Two

Aurora

I shield my eyes and head toward the building as horns blare at me. Black smoke billows from the tall exhausts attached to the massive trucks. A truck stop isn't exactly the safest place for a girl on her own, but what choice do I have? I'm trying to get across the country.

I was born in New York, but I chose to attend college in California. So many brazen dreams and wild hopes filled my head then, and for the first few semesters, things were fine. I did well in my classes and though I mostly kept to myself, I had a budding social life. Yes, things were just fine.

Until they weren't.

My parents believe I've graduated and am living my best life because that's what I told them the last time we spoke. In reality, I dropped out and have been on a steady decline. I stopped answering their calls, and once my phone was stolen, avoiding them became the least of my worries.

I have no source of steady income, and I'm down to a

measly twenty, ten of which I'm about to spend so I can take a hot shower. To make more money, I'll have to go on "dates." What little I earn quickly dwindles away once I pay for food and showers. At least the rides from one truck stop to the next are free. Well, I guess they aren't, since I technically pay for them with my body.

Jazz music floats from the overhead speakers the moment I step through the glass doors and enter the truck stop. I stop and listen to the familiar tune and realize it's a gaudy rendition of "Careless Whisper." Now I feel like I'm in an elevator filled with racks of snacks and coolers of beer and soda.

Gripping the backpack strap digging into my right shoulder, I meander toward the counter, where an elderly woman peers at me beneath a mess of white curls. The way her pinched lips curve inward, I can tell she has no teeth. Or if she does, there aren't enough left to push her mouth into a proper shape.

"I need a shower," I say as I slide a ten across the counter.

She lifts the bill and holds it up to the light, then opens the register drawer and slides the money inside. A receipt prints out, and she hands it to me. "The code's on there. Don't dillydally, and we don't allow men and women in there together."

I normally say thank you because it's just good manners, but this old hag can go choke on her remaining teeth for all I care. Sex work is work, and her judgment isn't needed.

Clutching the short strip of paper in my hand, I head toward the showers so I can wash away the travel grime. I punch the code into the keypad, and the door unlocks. Once I'm inside, I fasten the deadbolt and turn toward the shower without looking in the mirror. I don't want to see myself right now. I don't want to see myself until I'm clean, when my wavy auburn hair isn't slick with grease and my clothes aren't sticky with sweat.

I'm looking forward to this shower way more than anything. If someone gave me the choice between a steak dinner and a ten-minute shower, I'd ignore the growl of my stomach and head straight for the running water.

There's only one downside to showers, which is all the thinking I'll do while I mindlessly wash myself.

I step beneath the water, and thoughts begin to circle my mind like the cloudy mess circling the shower drain. Why am I even heading home? To come face to face with my parents' disapproving looks? They think I'm this very successful twenty-four-year-old political student graduate, but in reality, I'm a whore. There's no other way to describe what I do. When they find out the truth . . .

Warm water slides down my back, gliding over a bruise on my left shoulder. The last trucker got a little too rough, but I've been through worse. Thankfully, not all the men are mean. The super truckers are a whole different breed. They're the kind of men who live and breathe trucking. They take care of themselves, they take care of their trucks, and for the most part, they're very respectful.

The last guy was not a super trucker.

I stick my hand beneath the shampoo dispenser and collect the gel in my palm. Rubbing my hands together, I form a lather and run it through my hair. Grime collects within the suds and flows down my body, taking the weight of the world with it as well.

I feel more human when I'm clean. More like myself. For this moment, I'm alive and healthy, despite the clenching hunger in my gut. I can ignore that gnawing pang, close my eyes, and pretend I'm at home, just taking a normal shower.

I can pretend the incident in my dorm never happened.

I can pretend I have loving and understanding parents.

I can pretend I graduated and became an advisor at the state department or joined some up-and-coming politician's team.

I can pretend I'm safe.

A girl can dream, can't she? It's the least I can do before returning to the nightmare of my harsh reality.

Once I've scrubbed my skin raw and rinsed away all the soap, I step out of the shower and look at myself in the mirror. The light has dimmed in my green eyes, and tiny red veins thread through my sclera. I've lost weight. A little too much, at that. I turn away from the mirror and grab my backpack. I don't want to look anymore.

My fingers dig through fabric until I find a clean jean skirt and a shirt that's a little too big for me now. I miss my fuller figure. Like a typical woman, I see the beauty in myself only after time has passed and changed me once again.

My eyes land on the shirt and shorts I discarded on the floor before my shower, and a decision begs to be made. I have enough money left to buy a little food, or I can wash my dirty clothes. Most people don't have to choose between eating and cleanliness. I wish I were most people.

With a sigh, I gather the clothes and stuff them into the side pocket with the rest of the shirts and shorts and panties that will have to wait until I make enough to clean them. I'm not even sure this truck stop has a laundry area anyway. Not all of them do. But I know they have an attached diner. I smelled the chicken grease as soon as I walked in.

After drying off my body, I dress and exit the shower

room. Once I've eaten a cheap meal to stave off the gnawing feeling in my gut, I'll need to scope out the lot for my next patron. And my next ride. I can't stay where I am forever, even if I'm not entirely sure where I'm headed. The plan has always been to travel toward home.

But sometimes plans change.

Chapter Three

Jax

I can only think of one thing as I take a seat at the bar in the truck stop's diner: Kane was—*is*—out of control. There's only so much I can do to stop his homicidal tendencies. He's fucked up and I'll be the first to admit that, but he's gone through things no child should. That's why he created me. Not *just* me, either.

When I can't break through, I try to stop him by derailing his thoughts, which is ultimately an impossibility. He becomes so hyper-focused on his rage that by the time I realize what's happening, by the time I feel the excitement and the dopamine, it's too late. He's already committed yet another homicide. He's done what he's done, and there's no taking it back.

Even if I could somehow stop him, that would mean his victim would live, and that creates a different problem entirely. If they live, they'll turn him in. As his protector, I have an obligation to protect Kane—to protect all three of us—and that means I can't step in once he's gone to a certain point. Which is fine, since I usually don't know what's happening until he's well past the point of no return.

While our system worked well in our youth, it isn't very effective now that he's an adult. I should have more control now, but Kane still holds the reins in a tight grip. And he shouldn't. Not until he gets ahold of himself.

A waitress approaches the counter. A few strands of bleached hair fall over her face, and she blows them away with a frustrated exhale. Dark bags under her eyes showcase just how tired she must be.

"What would you like to drink?" she asks.

"Coffee and water, please," I say.

She offers a curt nod and turns toward the coffee machine sitting atop a grimy counter behind her. If her shuffling gait and the way she keeps rubbing her lower back are any indication, she's probably been on shift all day. She grabs a faded red cup and fills it with water. No ice. Instead of bothering her with another request, I let it go. The poor thing has enough to think about.

As I wait for the coffee—which has to be made, much to the waitress's displeasure—I spin around on the stool and study the pokey diner's sparse decor. Glossy red vinyl covers the bar stools, which are bolted to the floor in front of the counter. Some of the covers have ripped, revealing their yellowed foam innards. The red-plastic booths have seen better days as well. Scuffs and scratches from years of trucker butts scraping across them mark their once shiny surfaces.

Another trucker sits at one of the booths. He's double-fisting coffee mugs, and I understand him. When you work for a company, you have to stick to the hours of service, including mandatory ten-hour breaks. Technically, we're all supposed to stick to that, but when you drive for yourself or a lackadaisical company, there's pressure to fudge your logs and keep driving. That guy looks like he's done more than a bit of fudging.

The waitress brings over my lukewarm water and a mug of fresh coffee. As I pull the glass toward me, I motion her closer before she can speed away. "Can I pay for his meal?" I ask, jerking my head toward the trucker in the booth.

She nods and trudges over to him to let him know. He leans back with an appreciative grunt and raises one of the coffee mugs toward me. I lift my glass of room-temperature water back at him, then continue scanning the diner.

An older couple sits at the other end of the counter, each of them picking away at a plate full of greasy food. I don't see that kind of relationship very often in my line of work, but they're more common these days. Couples who travel together. It would be nice to have someone to share the lonely hours on the road with, but Kane wouldn't let it last very long. His house, his rules.

I'm about to turn back to my coffee when a young woman catches my eye. She sticks out in a place like this. Her legs are crossed, causing her jean skirt to ride up her thighs, and her wet hair hangs over her shoulders, dampening her shirt. One sleeve falls from her shoulder and reveals several small bruises. The way they form a line, it almost looks like fingers gripped her there.

Maybe they did.

She imprints on my memory, and I know Kane can sense my physical attraction to her because he knocks at the mental image. That's how it works for us. He can't see her through my eyes, but he can see the vision I've burned into my brain. Well, *our* brain.

Kane comes through as a burning behind my eyes. An intensity that sears the nerves resting close to my brain. I wish he'd let it go. He just fucking killed a girl. He doesn't need to come out and take another so soon. But the knocking gets harder. As he throws his consciousness against the mental barrier, I know it's only a matter of time before I'm pushed out of the driver's seat. I have no control over this. None of us do.

I just want to sit here and enjoy my coffee.

As I grip the warm mug, I search for something else to focus on. Fractured lines run through the glass, but they don't compromise its integrity. From the looks of things, this place plans to hold on to each aged item until it's broken past the point of usefulness. I continue staring at the cracks in the glass, counting every line branching from the main fracture as I try to will Kane away.

I squint my eyes as I pour creamer and a hint of sugar into my mug. I bring it to my mouth and take a small sip. It's the same trash coffee I've gotten used to at places like this. The same bitter bite. The same hint of something left over from the last twenty unwashed pots that have come before this one.

The burning behind my eyes intensifies, regardless of how I try to pretend it doesn't. Usually we communicate with notes. Very rarely do our thoughts overflow into each other. But this time, on this night, they do.

I need her, he whispers.

It's not his voice, though. It's mine. But it's not my thought. It comes from some nefarious place that isn't part of me, even though it's inside me.

No, Kane. Leave her, I respond in my head. I don't know if he can hear me, but even if he can, he'll likely ignore me.

I guess he doesn't like that answer, because an explosion ricochets through my mind. My heart gallops and my vision blurs until the whole diner becomes abstract. I'm losing control. Kane is taking over. And he'll hurt that poor girl, all because I took a liking to her.

Sweat gathers on my temples as each breath grows sharper. I drop the mug and it spills hot coffee all over my lap before it skitters off the counter and shatters on the diner floor.

Chapter Four

Aurora

Shattering glass draws my attention. The sound is brief, but it's enough to overpower the low clatter and hum of the diner. A man sits at the counter, his lap covered in coffee. The shards of a white mug litter the ground beneath his stool. His eyes scour the counter, likely searching for paper towels or napkins as the liquid sinks into his jeans, but the only napkin holder at the counter is empty, and the rest are spread across the restaurant.

I grab a stack of napkins from the dispenser at my table and bring them to him. He takes the crinkled sheets of tan paper and brings them to his shirt, dabbing at the material before turning his focus to his jeans.

"Thanks," he says, a bit of a southern twang in his deep voice. His dark eyes move up my body before he turns away without saying another word.

He seems completely disinterested in conversation, and I feel pretty awkward just standing here, so I back away. I did my good deed for the day.

I settle back in my seat and stare at the empty tabletop. I've been here for a while without so much as a nod from any staff. The waitress finally spots me now that I've been to the counter and back, and she approaches my table and asks what I'd like.

What I'd like is a steak dinner, complete with a baked potato, side salad, and a glass of Moscato, but I doubt I could even afford the potato at this point. After the cost of my shower, I might have enough for some oil-burned fries and a drink. My stomach growls at the thought of anything edible.

"A small order of fries and a small Coke," I say.

The disappointment in my tone must be really apparent, because Mr. Friendly looks over at me from the counter. "Give her whatever she wants," he calls across the restaurant.

"Excuse me?" I say.

"Order whatever you want. On me."

I shake my head at the waitress despite the utter protest of my stomach. That bitch says I'd drop to my knees for a meal at this point. "The fries are fine."

"Girl, if you want a goddamn steak, get it," the man says.

I swallow. "No, really, I—"

"Consider it my thank you."

The waitress shifts her weight on her white-sneakered feet, clearly growing impatient with our argument. Before I can say anything else, he places a wad of bills on the counter, stands up, and heads for the door.

A bell dings overhead as he exits the diner, and I can't help but stare through the dirt-streaked window as he makes his way across the parking lot. His jeans hang low, and a nice leather belt keeps them from dropping off his waist. Heavy black boots peek beneath his crisp pant legs with each step he takes, and a flannel shirt hugs his muscled arms. He moves like an animal stalking through grass, somehow slow and fast at the same time. Somehow . . . kind of sexy.

The man stops beside the fanciest truck I've ever seen and climbs inside. From the shape of the tractor, I can tell it houses an extended sleeper. I've only been inside one like that, and this one is even bigger. I can't help but wonder what the bed is like inside. I'm sick of low, shitty bunk beds.

I bet it's comfortable.

And clean.

The waitress clears her throat, and I turn toward her. I feel bad for making her wait, but I feel even worse about taking the guy's money. Then again, he's already left the building and it would be a real shame to let that money go to waste.

Fuck it.

"I'd like a steak, please, with a baked potato if you have any."

The waitress walks away.

I go back to staring out the window as I wait for my food. The man helps a little brown dog out of his truck, gripping the thin leash in his hand as he leads the furry creature toward a small patch of grass. A few of the truckers I've met have had pets on the road with them, and most of their personalities match the type of pet they own. I expected someone like him to have a Doberman or some sort of shepherd. But no, this little fluffy dog sticks close to his side as they walk toward the grass. It looks kind of like a Pomeranian mix.

The only Pomeranian I've ever met was this dog a girl in my class brought as an emotional support animal. I don't know how much emotional support he provided. He was a yappy little ankle biter who would quite happily shit on your pillow if you let him into your dorm room. This man's dog is the complete opposite. It seems well-mannered and quiet.

Thoughts of that Pomeranian in the dorms send my mind to dangerous places. I wish I hadn't gone right to college after high school. Then running away from college just brought me to truck stops where I'm forced to get on my knees for a meal. It seems I've been running from things my entire life. Now I have nowhere else to run to.

And nowhere to sleep.

I've usually been asked to go on a date by now, but it's too quiet tonight. There aren't many trucks in the lot, and the guy who bought my dinner didn't seem very interested. Once I've finished my steak, I'll have to get out there and weasel my way into someone's good graces. Hopefully, they'll be as nice as the guy in the purple truck.

Chapter Five

Kane

While she sits inside and eats her meal, I wait in my truck. That girl sure is a pretty little thing. Modest too. She didn't even want to accept the favor. I can see why Jax took a liking to her.

And why he tried so hard to keep me away.

No one can hold me back from something I really want, though, and especially not when what I want looks that good in a tight little jean skirt. Poor Jax really put up a fight to stay in control for her sake, but he's just not strong enough.

I don't really talk much about my alters because I consider them nuisances. They always seem to come knocking when I don't want them to. Though their intentions are usually good, they can fuck right off about this. *This* is my life. My hobby. What I enjoy doing. I'm a forty-year-old man, so I figure they should be used to this by now. What I do. What *we* do. They can try to separate themselves from me all they want, but they are a part of me.

My fucking family. Estranged, but family all the same.

Jax is the sweet brother I needed.

Tobin is the pesky sibling I never wanted.

There are others as well, but Jax and Tobin are the two who come around most often. They're the main contenders fighting for space in my brain. I've gained some and lost some over the years, but those two have remained consistent —consistent pains in my ass.

But I need them.

They hold the keys to the doors I can't open. They hide the things that would hurt me and make me more dangerous than I am now. What could be worse than a highly prolific interstate serial killer? I don't know. But I'd sure figure it out without them.

Some people believe that having alters makes me crazy. This couldn't be further from the truth. My alters strive to keep me sane. They compartmentalize the pain, allowing me to escape it. Well, most of it. Sometimes the pain is too great to be contained behind a door. Sometimes it seeps through the cracks.

Movement catches my attention, and I look toward the truck stop. The girl exits the building, looking satisfied after her meal. My eyes lock on her, and a foggy haze falls over my mind. Someone wants to take over and put this truck in drive. They urge me to leave her behind.

But I focus on my breathing and tell him no.

He can't keep me from her. No one can. Not even the person created to protect me from all the pain can keep me from inflicting so much hurt on someone else.

Pup whines beside me before settling on the seat. I reach over and pat her head while keeping my eyes glued to the girl walking toward the parking lot. Something about her seems broken. Not quite as broken as some of these bitches out here, but she's experienced some amount of damage.

It's not that I care, though. These are just observances. Things I notice. Whatever damaged her in the past will be child's play compared to what I plan to do to her.

The young girl looks around the parking lot. She wraps her arms around herself as the breeze whips her auburn hair behind her. After studying the few trucks lined up on the side of the building, she starts toward the entrance to the highway. Her thumb goes into the air when she reaches the road, but she spares one more glance toward the trucks.

She knows what she's doing. This is her signal, letting men like me know she's open for business.

The nag behind my eyes can fuck off. She's placed herself on a silver platter, and I'm ready to eat. She's the one being stupid, walking around like a prime cut of meat in a market full of starved truckers. I won't even have to abduct this one. She'll willingly climb into my truck, especially after that sweet gesture from me.

I turn the key, and the engine roars to life. The mechanical sound fills the silence as I put it in gear and drive toward the highway entrance. My brakes depressurize as I pull up to a stop beside her, creating a loud hiss. I look into her pretty eyes as I roll down my window.

"You need a ride too?" I yell over the rumble of my truck.

She looks around, unsure whether she should take a ride from me. She has good intuition and every right to be concerned. Hitchhikers are my favorite kind of girl to grab. They typically come from nowhere, and with nowhere to be, they're an excellent target.

The knock in my head recedes to a dull tap. Jax knows

it's too late. The trap has been set, and she's already nibbling on the bait.

She bites her bottom lip before answering me. "Yeah, I guess I do."

"Hop in." I move Pup to the floor between the seats.

The girl climbs into my rig, and her skirt rides up her thighs as she situates herself in the passenger seat. Pup stands on her back legs to get to the girl. She has this terrible habit of biting anyone who isn't me, including Tobin. I open my mouth to scold her before she scares the girl off, but I'm stunned to silence when Pup licks her arm instead of sinking her needle teeth into her skin.

"What's her name?" she asks as she strokes the fluff behind Pup's ears.

"Pup."

"Hello, Pup," she coos, her hand disappearing beneath the long fur.

The girl looks toward my sleeper. A small galley stands in the middle, complete with a sink and microwave. Further back, there's a flatscreen TV and a couch seat that turns into a tabletop for dinners. Dark cabinets hovering above the full-sized bed provide storage. I paid for all the bells and whistles, and it's been worth every fucking penny.

"What's your name?" I ask, drawing her gaze back to me.

"Aurora."

"Kane," I say, even though she didn't bother to ask. "Why's a pretty girl like you hanging out with truckers like us?"

Her shoulders lift in a shrug. "I go on dates with them."

My eyebrow rises. "*That* kind of date?"

"Yeah," she whispers.

She's not a lot lizard. She's much too young and pretty

to be called that yet, but after a few more years in this line of work, she'll fit right in. I'm glad I've gotten to her before her shiny veneer has been rubbed away.

"How much do you charge?" I ask. And why the fuck not? What else would I ask someone like her?

"The standard. Forty-sixty-eighty."

"I don't usually pick up girls like you, so I'm not sure what the standard means." This is a lie. I pick up girls just like her all the time. And then I bury them. I've heard it all before, but I want to hear her young, sweet little mouth say those filthy words.

"Forty for oral, sixty for sex, or eighty if you want both. If you only want a hand job, I could do twenty."

She speaks so transactionally, like a businesswoman. She's not like the others, though. Instead of pawing at my lap to convince me to buy what she's selling, she knows what she's got and she doesn't need to get pushy. Unfortunately for her, I have no use for her product, even though the outer packaging makes my mouth water. It's like charging a toothless man for a roasted and buttered ear of corn; he'd love to eat it, but he can only slobber all over it and make a mess.

Her green eyes harden on me. "Did you want anything?"

"Nah, not at the moment."

A look of rejection crosses her face. She doesn't understand why I'm turning her down, and I don't have the desire to explain myself. Even if I could get hard, I ain't paying for it. Besides, I need to get a few more miles under my belt before I play with her the way I want to.

Her fingers move toward the door handle. My disinterest in fucking her seems to have made her suspicious. I'll need to lower her guard again.

My head cocks as I eye her. I can't do anything with her myself, but she's pretty enough to sell. Considering I still owe The Nameless for the purchase of this truck, maybe selling her would be better than killing her. She'd fetch a higher price than some of the others I've sold.

Most of the girls I've taken aren't worth The Nameless' time. They're too old or tired or unsightly, like knackered horses at the stockyard. So I get rid of them. On rare occasions, I run across a girl who's still got some light in her eyes. Like this one.

It's a double-edged sword. I'd prefer to kill all of them, but without my truck, I'm useless. I can't work, and I sure as shit can't continue my spree. This girl would knock down a good chunk of my debt, though, so I'll have to make a decision soon. Once I've driven her around a bit, I'll decide whether she'll end up with them or in a hole in the ground.

Honestly, the hole is probably the kinder option. The Nameless aren't cruel—wouldn't want to damage the merchandise—but they send the girls to people who do far worse than what I put them through.

Her fingers tighten on the handle, so I put the truck in gear and head toward the highway. We bounce in the fancy air seats as we hit potholes littering the on-ramp.

"Where you headed?" I ask, trying to get her to release the damn handle and sit the fuck back so I can drive without worrying she'll jump out of my truck. Women have tried before. Sheer desperation has a way of removing the fear of rolling across asphalt at seventy miles per hour.

"New York," she says, and I release a silent sigh of relief as her hand returns to her lap.

I head east, but I don't plan to stay on that course. Like purchasing that meal for her, this is just to lull her into a false sense of security until I get her handcuffed in the back.

Until then, I'll go the way she wants and keep her comfortable. I've got a tank full of diesel and all the time in the world.

That's part of my problem. I have too much time on my hands at the moment. I drive a reefer unit, which means I transport temperature-sensitive items in a refrigerated hold, but my supplier bailed at the last minute. A downside to being a private trucker is that I can't just whip up an order out of thin air like the drivers for the bigger companies can, but I sure as fuck couldn't kill while driving a company rig. Not easily, at least. In that way, it's a fair trade.

That huge loss in shipment is also why it would make more sense for me to sell her to The Nameless instead of putting her in the ground.

A group of brothers runs The Nameless, and I grew up with the oldest of the three. I call them The Nameless, but I know each of their names and what they're capable of. I've kept their business at arm's length, but when I had the opportunity to purchase this truck, I couldn't pass it by. I dipped a finger into their world, and I can't pull myself from their dirty dealings until I've paid them off.

I don't want to know any more about what they do than what I know now. I keep them nameless for a reason. Aside from the occasional business transaction, I want nothing to do with them. I bring them a bitch, and they carve a few chunks out of the debt I owe.

I eye the girl again and wonder just how much she'll go for. And if it's really worth it.

Chapter Six

Aurora

I glance at him as his powerful hands clutch the steering wheel. The little dog jumps into my lap and places its paws on the door so it can peer out the window. She's missing one of her front legs, but it doesn't seem to hinder her at all.

Kane and Pup. What an odd combination.

A few miles down the interstate, he pulls off his flannel shirt and tosses it onto the back of his seat. His white t-shirt rides up his taut abdomen. With his torso twisted and his head craned backward, I notice the word "Daddy" scrawled on his skin in traditional tattoo lettering. A tattoo like that would normally make me cringe, but this guy oozes the daddy vibe. Like he'd bend you over his lap and spank you while you call him that.

More tattoos paint his arm, peeking from beneath his shirtsleeves and traveling down to his wrists. I'd probably find him attractive if he weren't so grumpy. And if the hard set of his jaw didn't set off warning bells in my head. Unfortunately, I'm not very good at listening to the warning bells. I have a bad habit of waiting until they've become blaring sirens.

I almost got out of the truck before we took off. When he said he wasn't interested in my services, that was somehow more unsettling than if he'd tried to rip off my clothes. The drivers are usually more than happy to get me underneath them as soon as possible. This one? He seems like he couldn't be less interested.

I suppose he might be a nice person who wants to give me a ride, but that feels highly unlikely. No one is nice just to be nice these days.

Clearing my throat, I try to think of something to talk about to ease the growing tension in my gut. "Which company do you work for?" I ask. "Not a lot of companies let people take pets along or pick up hitchhikers."

"I don't work for a company. I work for myself."

Conversing with him is like fucking myself with a dildo. I'm forced to do all the work. I try to think of a question that would force him to talk a little more. Private drivers aren't very common, and I've never gotten in a truck that didn't belong to a big company, so I decide to stick with that line of questioning.

"Why do you drive private?" I ask.

"I'm a felon," he says without breaking eye contact with the road. But it's still a short answer, and now I'm intrigued.

"What did you do time for?"

"Mind your questions, girl."

The stern way he speaks is exactly what I mean when I say he has a daddy vibe. It's the type of tone that makes you shut the fuck up real quick, but there's also an edge of something sinister to his words. My fingers move toward the door handle again, and I seriously consider leaping from the rig and onto the interstate. It wouldn't be the first time I've leaped from a moving vehicle, though it wasn't moving anywhere near this fast.

I take a deep breath and force myself to calm down and remember the clientele I've chosen to associate with. Most are gruff. Most aren't big on talking. And more are unsavory than not.

So far, they've just gotten a little rough with me, but I've always been able to handle myself. My father was a long-haul trucker for most of my life. Then my mother wanted him to settle down, so he gave it up so he could be home every night.

I liked my father better when he was a trucker than when he was retired. Alcohol became his crutch once he was home every day, and he's a nasty drunk. But because of him, I'm more comfortable around truckers than I am with other random men, so that's why I'm a truck stop whore. Well, that's what other people call me. I call myself a working girl. These are merely my dates—a way to eat, sleep, and eventually go back home.

Eventually.

We're currently in Ohio, and I don't know how far he'll take me. Or how long I'm willing to ride with him. I still don't know what he wants from me, and I'm not sure I could handle the unease for more than a day or two.

Maybe he's not even attracted to me. Maybe he's just a nice guy who will drop me off at the next truck stop and I won't have to think about any of this. But then again, nice guys aren't often felons with *Daddy* tattooed on their necks.

To my left, Kane rubs his eyes with the back of his hand and blinks a few times. I have to do a double take, because he looks . . . different. I can't quite put my finger on what's changed, but something about his face isn't quite the same as it was before. His jaw is still as clenched as ever, and he's the same person, but somehow not.

"Are you okay?" I ask.

He clears his throat and rubs his eyes again. "Just a headache."

Well, I guess I'm imagining things, because his answers are just as short and gruff as before.

I settle in my seat and stroke the dog in my lap as the road signs pass by in a blur of headlights. My eyelids try to close, but I will them to remain open. It's not safe to sleep. Not yet. Not until I know he won't pull over and murder me the first chance he gets. This is the risk I take each time I climb inside a stranger's home. And that's exactly what these trucks are for most of these men.

Even if they have a wife back in a little two-bedroom apartment, they spend too much time in these rigs to not see them as a house on wheels. I think that's why some of them choose this line of work. They can live two lives. Meanwhile, I'm struggling to live *one.*

And I'm doing a piss-poor job.

It wasn't supposed to be this way. I was a girl with dreams once, just like anyone else. Those dreams changed along the way, but I still have them. A desire to belong somewhere. A desire to feel safe. I doubt I'll find either of those things if I continue walking along the path I'm on, so that's why I'm headed home.

Is that even the answer?

I push the thought away as soon as it forms. Now isn't the time to think about that. To keep myself sane, I have to live in the moment and focus on the immediate threat, which is a large man who is mere feet from me. As he rubs his eyes again and keeps his focus on the road, I can't help but wonder if I've made a mistake that may cost me my life.

Chapter Seven

Tobin

The number combo rolls through my head as I take control. *Forty. Sixty. Eighty.* I can't stop thinking about it. Even when I was behind Kane, listening to her talk through his ears, those three numbers taunted me. Even without seeing her, I knew I wanted all fucking eighty.

Since he picked her up, Kane's thoughts have circled back to all the horrific ways he could kill her. Filet pieces of muscle from bone. Chop off limbs until she stops screaming. Hold her head beneath water until she stops struggling. All after he strangles her first, of course.

But I don't care about the killing. I give zero fucks about that. My mind just keeps repeating those glorious numbers.

Forty. Sixty. Eighty.

He won't kill her, though. It might bring him great joy to end her young life, but he knows damn well he needs to sell this one to The Nameless. The sooner he gets out from under their thumbs, the sooner he can kill whomever he pleases. And if he isn't going to kill her, if she's stuck with us until we deliver her to The Nameless . . .

Forty. Sixty. Eighty.

A sign for a rest stop slides by on the right side of the road, and I inhale. Kane let me drive so easily. Instead of fighting me this time, he just let go so I could take control. It was a smart decision on his part. Until he sells her to The Nameless, she's useless to him.

But she's not useless to me.

Kane was sexually abused as a child, and I hold all those nasty memories for him. The pain. The suffering. The fear. As a result, I'm a hyper-sexualized consciousness born from sexual trauma. I can explore the aspects of lust Kane has become immune to. Though his brain has compartmentalized those painful memories, his body has forgotten nothing, rendering him limp any time he attempts sexual acts. Unlike Kane, I have no trouble getting hard.

Now I realize why he let me take control.

The girl is suspicious, and the only way to ease her mind is to sleep with her. If she tries to manhandle our junk while Kane is in control, she'll learn the truth. It would also send him into a blind rage, and he'd bludgeon her to death before he could sell her off. I suppose a limp dick would make me homicidal too.

I pull onto the off ramp and enter the rest area. Dim lights limn the building in a weak glow, and a few towering streetlamps illuminate the parking lot, but a back corner has been left in darkness. Looks like someone forgot to change the bulbs back here. Their irresponsibility is a benefit to me, and I pull into the darkest spot I can find.

I turn toward the girl and finally get a good look at her.

Kane had good taste for this one. Long, unruly auburn hair frames her face. Not too dark, not too light. She's not wearing any makeup, which is good. She doesn't need it. Her full lips are the perfect shade of pink, and her long lashes would look garish if she coated them in mascara.

"Forty, sixty, eighty, right?" I ask.

Her hands stop fidgeting in her lap. "Yeah," she whispers.

"Get in the back."

She takes a breath, unlocks her seatbelt, and climbs out of the seat. She knows the drill. With an air of confidence possessed only by a whore who's ready to lie on her back, she heads right for the bed. Unfortunately for her, it doesn't matter if I take her mouth, pussy, or both. I'll get what I want, and I won't pay for shit.

I unbuckle my seatbelt and stand to follow her. As I stretch, the bratty little dog nips at my ankles with a growl that rattles her tiny body. Mean little mutt. Why Kane wanted this annoying thing is beyond me, but he loves the little shit. He won't outwardly say it, but I feel the warmth for the dog in his heart. It's one of the few fleshy spots left inside the dying organ. The rest is black, decayed, and stinking.

"Fuck off, little dog," I say as I pull the denim from her mouth.

Before I can join the girl, I notice a clutch peeking from a backpack on the seat. I pull it free and pop it open, and a picture of the girl smiles up at me from her driver's license.

Aurora Rivelle. Twenty-four. Albany, New York.

I flip past the ID and find a picture tucked beneath a flap. In it, she stands with a man and a woman—her parents, I presume—beside a truck similar to mine. She's a trucker's daughter? No wonder she's so comfortable getting into the rigs with us.

She'll regret that in the end.

"Are you coming?" she calls from the back.

Soon enough, I think with a smirk as I tuck the clutch into the backpack.

As I enter the back of the rig, she looks at me with sweet fuck-me eyes. That look will fade when I get my hands on her.

"What do you want?" she asks.

She wastes no time waiting for my answer, and her hand goes for my zipper. Her eyes widen as she pulls out my cock and sees my dick. I can't help but wonder if it's because of the length or girth. Maybe it's the black metal piercing or the tattoo etched into that sensitive area. *Cry for me,* it says.

Kane fucking flipped when he saw it. Women aren't able to cry for him when he can't even get hard, so I think it hurt his delicate ego a bit. He shouldn't worry. He might be incapable of sexual intimacy, but I'm primed to provide our body with what it needs.

I grip her chin, and she whimpers. "Your mouth. And your dirty whore cunt," I growl.

"Eighty," she says, squeezing her eyes closed against the pain of my pinching grasp.

"You got a meal for free. A ride. With the price of fuel these days, I'd say we're about even, little girl."

Her eyes open. "You have to pay me. I need the money."

"You won't need anything with us."

"Us?"

"Me," I blurt, trying to correct my mistake.

I sometimes forget that to people like her, to everyone

else, we're just Kane. It doesn't matter who's driving at the time. And that's the shitty part of this setup because I'm *not* him. I'm *me*, my own person living inside his fucked-up little mind. I matter too. I have my own desires and wants and needs. I'm my own person.

She tries to scramble away, but I grab her arm and tug her back to me.

"If you cause me any trouble, Ms. Rivelle, I'll personally pay a visit to your family on Carnation Road."

Her widening gaze shifts to the passenger seat as she realizes I've looked at her ID. Girls like her don't typically have caring parents, which also means the girls don't care about the parents. She's a unique one, though. As soon as I saw the picture, I knew I had a whore with a heart. That's a detriment in her line of work, though. It gives me all the ammo I need.

"Fuck you," she says, and I'm surprised by how calm she is.

I smirk. She's something else. And I kind of like it.

I push her onto the bed but turn away and head to the kitchen instead of leaping on her. I pull two bottles of beer from the small fridge, pop them open, and offer one to her.

"Drink," I say.

She eyes the bottle for a moment before tipping it against her lips and emptying it as quickly as I empty mine. A line of escaped alcohol dribbles from the corner of her mouth, and she wipes it away with the back of her hand, her eyes never leaving mine.

I take a step back and lick my lips. "Now fuck yourself with it."

Most girls get weird about using objects, acting as if they never experimented with things when they were younger.

Not Aurora, though. She spreads her legs, giving me a view of everything beneath her short skirt as she grips the bottle's base. Her hand moves to her pussy, and as she spreads the full lips, I can't help but harden. It's such a good-looking cunt.

She swirls her tongue around the mouth of the bottle, lubricating the glass before she lowers it to her entrance and pushes it inside. She hooks her arm around her thigh and thrusts in and out, but she doesn't moan or make a sound. Even as she fucks herself harder, she remains silent. When she pulls it out and sucks it into her mouth, I nearly come in my pants.

"Why are you fucking yourself so good for me, little whore?"

"Because I'm not trying to be any trouble," she says with a snarky hiss in her tone.

She changes positions, getting onto her hands and knees as she faces her ass toward me. Resting her head on the bed, she positions the bottle between her thighs and continues to fuck herself. I can't keep my hand off my cock as I watch her. With every push of the bottle, my hand matches the speed and strength. But it's not enough.

"Keep playing with yourself, but give me your mouth," I command.

When she doesn't move, I fist her hair and pull her face to my cock. Her upper lip curls in a snarl before she relents and opens her mouth. My skin sings with pleasure as I push my cock into her warm mouth, and I don't go easy on her. I force myself to the back of her throat because a seasoned whore like her can take every inch of me. She's a goddamn professional.

The writing along my dick disappears and reappears as

I fuck her mouth. Her eyes water, and a tear slips down her cheek.

"Yes. Cry for me. Just like my dick says."

Tears stream down her cheeks. I give her a hard smack, yet she hardly reacts to it. I'm confused by her lack of fight, but I don't need it to get off. I'm a deviant, not a rapist. In fact, I love that she isn't fighting me.

It won't save her, though. I don't have that power. I'm just enjoying her while I can.

She pulls away from me, and I allow it. "Are you going to fuck me or what? Just get it over with."

"If you want to skip to the fun part, that's fine with me."

And it is. It doesn't bother me that she's treating this as a transaction. She doesn't have to fight for me to enjoy it, but she doesn't have to be into it either. It might be more pleasant for her if she was, but I don't mind using her body if she's not.

I flip her over, pull the bottle from her pussy, and replace it with my cock. The ink along my dick disappears inside her. I should use a condom with a whore, but I want to feel what the bottle felt. Something inanimate shouldn't get to experience something I can't.

She whimpers as my piercing rakes her pussy walls, and it's the first reaction out of her aside from her mouthy words. I grip her hair and lift her, and she screams out.

"Kane," she whimpers.

I want to tell her Kane isn't here and she should be glad, but I don't. "You were the one who wanted to skip ahead. I'd tell you not to cry, but I like your tears. I like them so much that I inked it into my fucking skin."

I wrap my hand around her throat and feel Kane behind the motions. His desire to kill rivals my desire to fuck, but I knock him back. I'm too close, and I won't let him rob me of this.

I fuck her harder, thrusting into her with as much force as I can muster. She becomes a whimpering, screaming mess in front of me. There's no way she's enjoying this, but I sure as fuck am.

"Where do the other johns come?" I ask, because I know it's coming.

Sweat and tears mingle on her face as she turns her head and answers me. "Inside me. But with a condom."

I chuckle. "Well, I'm not using a condom, but I'll still come inside you."

"Don't!" she cries.

But I do. I come deep inside her, with every word of my tattoo buried within her cunt. But I'm not done with her. I want to savor our mess.

I pull out and press the lip of the bottle to her entrance. "Push it out."

She bears down and the come drips into the bottle. And it's a lot. Her pussy was incredible, so I'm not surprised.

With a flick of my wrist, I swirl the mixture of beer and come around the bottom of the bottle as I go to the fridge and remove the empty ice tray. I've been meaning to fill this, but I'm glad I forgot until now. I put a little water into the bottle and swirl again before filling what few empty rectangles I can. Then I fill the right half of the tray with normal water.

As I slide the tray into the freezer compartment, a thought hits me. If Kane and Jax take any from the left side, they'll kill me. Tobin, back at it again, fucking up our peaceful little system. I hate to tell them, but that ship has sailed. One third of the system is majorly homicidal, the other is a sexual deviant, and the remainder isn't strong enough to bring the peace we need. Besides, with the way Kane kills, the least of our problems is some come-laced ice cubes in the freezer.

As the backs of my eyes begin to burn, I grab a bag of chips and return to the front of the truck. Now that my job is done, someone else wishes to take the helm for a bit. I wonder who she'll have to deal with next. For her sake, I hope it isn't Kane.

Chapter Eight

Aurora

I fix my skirt without shame, lowering the hem to its proper position and turning it the right way around again. Shame isn't really in my vocabulary anymore, though I suppose it should be. How I use my body—or rather, how I allow others to use my body—is certainly deemed as shameful by a large chunk of the population. But I'm willing to bet those individuals haven't been through what I've been through. They judge through rose-colored glasses. I stare through unprotected eyes.

We are not the same.

Though I've had some odd interactions with my clientele since starting this line of work, what just happened wasn't the strangest. Not even close. Fucking myself with a beer bottle was small beans compared to the men who've paid extra for me to piss on their chests or shit on their stomachs. Some have even asked to do the same to me, though I politely declined. We all have our hard limits.

That brings my mind back around to payment, a subject he seems to have no interest in revisiting. The food and the ride aren't payment enough, and he offered those things without mentioning reimbursement. If he'll just pay what he owes, I won't even bother with my kink add-on fee.

As I walk to the front of the truck, I spot a Post-it note on the fridge. I didn't notice it before, but then again, I wasn't exactly admiring the decor when I made my way back here. On the little square piece of paper, a singular sentence has been scrawled in blocky letters.

I FUCKED HER
-TOBIN

Who the fuck is Tobin? Didn't he say his name was Kane?

With more questions than answers—and an increasing sense of unease building in my gut—I muster the courage to press the payment issue. Once I have the cash in my hand, I'm getting out of here. I can hitch a ride to the nearest truck stop. Someone is bound to stop by this rest area.

Eventually.

By the time I reach the front, he's back in the driver's seat, a small bag of chips in his hands. With hungry eyes, Pup watches each triangular morsel travel to his mouth. He tosses her a chip, and I take that to mean he's in a better mood.

"Can I have my money now?" I ask.

Putting the bag of chips between his teeth, he pulls a weathered wallet from his back pocket and eases four twenties from the stack of bills inside.

"Sorry about that," he mumbles past the cellophane as I accept the cash.

Now I'm a bit confused. I expected some pushback, especially after he so brazenly threatened my family, but his willingness to pay up isn't the strangest part. It's his voice.

When I first met him, he'd been gruff. In the back of the truck just now, he'd seemed almost gruffer, if that's even possible. He'd certainly been more demanding. But now? Now he sounds almost nice. His tone isn't as sharp, there isn't as much of an edge to each word, and he seems genuinely apologetic about the whole payment debacle.

Is this guy bipolar?

In college, my roommate struggled with bipolar disorder. When she'd go off her medication for weeks at a time, she'd suffer from personality shifts that were abrupt enough to worry me. One minute she'd be happy as a pig in shit, and the next she'd be screaming about how messy my side of the room was. When she finally broke down and explained her condition, I understood her so much more. But something about this doesn't quite fit.

For starters, her voice, facial expressions, and mannerisms weren't so drastically different. Whether she was manic, depressed, or somewhere in the middle, she was still the same person. This guy is more like night and day. Antarctica and Africa. Soup and steak.

This solidifies my decision. It's time to get the hell out of here.

"I'm going to go now," I say, looking around the front passenger seat for my backpack.

He stands and places a hand on my shoulder. The touch is gentle, not at all forceful, and his eyes radiate a sadness that stops my search. "That's not possible, Aurora. He—" Kane sucks in a breath. "You can't leave."

"Sure I can," I say. "Just give me my things and I'll get

out of your hair. You'll never hear from me again. That's a promise."

He shakes his head. "It's not that simple."

"No, it's not that complicated. You paid me. I have no issue with you. If you're concerned about what you had me do back there, don't be. Keeping kinky secrets is part of the job description."

I try to force a smile and appear calm, but it's difficult when my heart is trying to beat out of my chest.

"I wish I could let you leave, sweet girl, but it's out of my hands," he whispers, lowering his gaze. "I never wanted to take you in the first place."

Take me? So it's as bad as I feared.

I make a run for the door handle, which is so stupid because the space is too small to escape his reach. His hand wraps around my arm, and my eyes clench shut as I anticipate the fist that will strike me or the fingers that will cinch around my throat. But he does neither of these things. Instead, he pulls me to his body, holding me against him as I struggle to break free. I'm uselessly expending energy—he could hold me like this all day without tiring, judging by the way his muscles bulge against my skin—so I still.

He tosses the bag of chips onto the dashboard, and his free hand brushes the stray strands of hair from my sweat-coated cheeks. "You're such a pretty girl. I'm so sorry."

I rip away from his touch. "Fuck you! Stop playing these mind games with me!"

"It's not a mind game. You just found yourself in a . . . particular situation."

"How so, Kane?"

He takes a deep breath. "I'm not Kane. My name's Jax."

What. The. Fuck. "I don't understand."

"You got in the truck with Kane, but I'm Jax. And you

clearly met Tobin." He gestures toward the note on the fridge.

I sink to the passenger seat, my feet melting into the floor. The strength has been sapped from my body. My feet are lead weights attached to limp noodles. My hands refuse to listen as I scream for them to grip the door handle. My voice seems to be the only cooperative participant.

"Please explain," I say as I stare straight ahead.

He rubs the space between his eyes, shakes his head, then pinches the bridge of his nose before a long, pained exhale rushes past his parted lips. "We're different people with the same brain. I'm sorry," he says. His eyes darken and his tone deepens. "Get your ass in the back. Now."

His eyes seem to change shape as I'm looking at them. His lips draw tight, and his sharp jaw tenses. He's not the same person he was seconds before. I don't know how this is possible, but it is.

Confusion, fear, and adrenaline freeze me in place. I'm unable to follow his order, even if I wanted to. And I don't. If I go back there, it's unlikely I'll ever make it out of this truck alive.

His hand wraps around my arm again, but this time, it isn't a gentle tug. Powerful fingers dig into my muscles, and I'm helpless in his grasp. As he pulls me through the kitchen, his eyes land on the note and he growls at the words etched in black marker.

"Jax?" I whisper.

"Jax? What the fuck is he telling you?" he snaps as he throws me onto the bed. "Stay the hell back here and shut the fuck up. You aren't going anywhere, and you need to forget about whatever I said before."

His heated stare drops to the money in my hand, and he

rips it from my grasp. I reach for it, but he pushes my back onto the bed again before leaning over me.

"I don't owe you a goddamn thing, least of all an explanation, so don't ask anymore fucking questions. Don't speak at all. Don't even *breathe* too loud. Just stay back here and look pretty." He slaps the side of my cheek, his touch too soft to be considered assault but too rough to call it a love pat.

I don't move as he stands, nor as his heavy bootsteps recede toward the front of the truck. This isn't a conscious choice. It's a learned response. My body has experienced fear before. It's an old friend, though it's paying me an unwelcome visit.

As I lie on this bed, my thoughts run in exhausting circles. He changed. Right in front of me, in the time it took to blink my eyes, he became a different person. This wasn't some act, either.

Time passes in slow motion, but I finally dare to sit up. My gaze darts across the space that seemed so large before. Now I feel more like a grain of sand within the eye of a needle. There are no weapons to speak of, so defending myself is out of the question. The only windows back here are too small to squeeze through, meaning my only exit is through the front.

Past him.

I lick my lips and lean to my right so I can peek at him. He's in the driver's seat, with his arms folded across his broad chest and his hat lowered over his eyes. He's settling in for a nap. How nice of him to give me the bed.

But how rude of him to fucking kidnap me. And that's exactly what this is. I've been kidnapped.

It shouldn't come as a surprise, but I never expected to find myself in this situation. I've tried to be careful. When people choose unregulated sex work, we understand the risks involved. We know we're all just one trick away from having our throats slit and our bodies dumped in an unmarked grave. It's all over the news. A few days ago, it was a girl from Portland. A month before that, it was a runaway teen from Spokane.

Today . . . it's me.

Chapter Nine

Kane

I pull the hat a little lower to block the glare of distant light as I lose myself to my thoughts. I don't know why Jax tried to explain this fucked-up situation we're in. He's got a little thing for the girl, I get it, but it's not his place to make her understand. She *can't* understand. No one ever does.

This goes deeper than trying to make her understand, though. Jax is the protector. The nurturing type. What I choose to do eats away at him, and he would have released that girl if his goal to protect our system didn't override his desire to protect things in general. But if he releases her, it puts all of us at risk. Deep down, he knows he needs to keep her right where she is so I can take care of what he can't.

We can't get caught.

Jax won't survive more prison time. I'd be fine, but he struggled when we were on the inside. Hell, even Tobin struggled, though his main complaint centered on the lack of pussy. From what the other inmates told me, I learned he combatted his desires by loudly jerking off every night. Though I will say, being so open about his sexual deviancy kept a *lot* of people away from us. Win-win. But Jax was a mess. He cried all the time. Imagine being known as the chronic masturbator and crier in one cell block. It wasn't a good look.

"Why are you giving me the bed?" she asks from the rear of the truck, and I don't even lift my hat from my face. I won't move unless she gives me a reason to.

"Go to sleep, dropout," I say. I let her take the bed so I could get a little shut-eye without worrying about her escaping.

"How do you know I'm a dropout?"

"I saw your college ID. I'm guessing a whore like you studied dicks instead of classwork."

When she scoffs and goes silent, I know I'm right.

Fabric scrapes against metal as she pulls the curtain across its track, separating us the only way she can. Is she planning an escape? Will I have to kill her here and now instead of handing her over to The Nameless?

The endless questions grind to a halt when gentle pressure lands against the front of my jeans. My torso jerks forward, and my hat falls to the floor as I escape her touch.

Abso-fucking-lutely not. I can't handle touch like that. Besides, she's just trying to butter me up so I'll lower my defenses and she can run off. That's also not happening.

My cock remains limp as can be, even as her big green eyes look up at me from her knees. Her hand moves toward me again, but I swat it away.

"Don't touch me," I say.

When she put her hand on me, it felt as if she'd wrapped her fingers around my throat instead of my dick. I don't remember why I have such a visceral reaction to touch.

My memories are black boxes in my mind. I know they're there, but there aren't labels or pictures to remind me of what waits beneath the locked lids, and I can't access their contents. Tobin has the keys. But even if my mind can't reach into those dark places and bring those memories into the light, my body recalls something about that touch.

The girl doesn't listen, though. She reaches for me again. Sweat slicks my skin and my heart thunders in my ears as my arm draws back. Before I know what's happening, I've backhanded her in the face. It's a knee-jerk reaction, that's all. If I wanted to hurt her, I'd have hit her with more than my hand.

She flies backward, and her back crashes against the leather passenger seat. "What the fuck!"

I shake my head and try to calm my breathing as I stare at her reddening cheek. I tried to warn her. She was told to stop, but words weren't convincing enough.

The backs of my eyes begin to burn, but I can't lose control right now. I *have* to set up this meeting with The Nameless, and that won't happen if I'm not in the driver's seat. Jax would be too busy hugging her and apologizing, and Tobin would just want to fuck her again.

I stand up and grip her by the hair as I lift her to her feet. "Don't fucking touch me like that. Don't *ever* touch me. Do you understand?"

Her fiery green eyes rise to mine as she struggles within my grasp. "But you can touch me?"

I didn't. I wouldn't. And I don't know how to explain that. There's absolutely no drive for me, and even if there was, it's not like I can perform.

"If I touch you, it's different," I snarl, "but don't initiate shit yourself. If I want to use your whore body, *I* will be the one to start it. If you try that again, the only thing you'll touch are the clods of earth I throw on your dead body."

That seems to drive the point home, and she stops struggling. "I need to pee," she whispers.

I let out a low growl, but I need to piss too. Keeping my hand within her hair, I drag her toward the passenger side door, pull the keyring from my pocket, and unlock the glove box. Within the compartment sits a beautiful 1911 with a wood grain grip. I like pretty things, what can I say?

I grab the gun and hold it in front of her face, keeping the barrel pointed toward the window. Safety first, after all. "If you run, I'll shoot you before you make it six feet from me. Allowing you to piss is a kindness. Do *not* mistake it for weakness. Do you understand?"

"Yes," she says.

I help her down from the truck, and she shifts her weight between her feet as if she's been holding her bladder for ages. This could all be another ploy, but I'll give her the benefit of the doubt for now. If she tries to run, she won't get very far with a bullet in her spine.

We walk toward the brick building squatting beside the parking lot. I keep her close to me as my mind works to sort through what I'm up against. Some rest areas staff attendants around the clock, but this building has already been locked up for the night. I can tell because the lights are off inside. The restrooms are on the outside—the men's room on the left and the women's room on the right. The lack of an attendant is a good thing. She can't scream for help, and I won't have to shoot two people instead of one. The distance between the two restrooms, though? Not great.

"Go in the men's room," I say as I stuff my pistol down

the back of my pants. I didn't see any cameras as we approached, but sometimes they're hidden well.

She sighs and walks into the men's room. I follow her until she's inside the stall, then I head to the urinal. When she starts to piss, I finally breathe a sigh of relief. Maybe she wasn't plotting after all.

The metal roll in her stall is already squeaking as she pulls paper from the holder before I've even finished. Before she can flush the toilet, I bear down on my bladder and piss a little faster.

The hinges squeal as the stall door opens, and she licks her lips as I look over my shoulder and meet her gaze. Then her eyes fall to my undone pants. Seeing an opportunity, the little bitch bolts for the restroom door.

"Fuck, fuck," I say beneath my breath. I shake droplets of urine from my cock and put it away so I can chase her. She can't escape. She's seen my truck. My face. And even though I didn't fuck her, I saw the note Tobin left behind, meaning she also has my DNA between her legs. Once it goes through CODIS, the great state of Ohio will issue a warrant.

I race out the door and scan my surroundings. It's dark out here, and even darker toward my truck and the woods just beyond. When footsteps crunch through dead leaves, I know which way she's gone.

And I follow.

"Stop now and I won't blow your brains all over this fucking rest stop, dropout!" I scream as I barrel toward the trees.

"Fuck you!" she yells back. She sounds so far away now, which means she's clearing ground faster than I can. I guess it makes sense. She's running for her life, and girls are so much faster when something that important is at stake.

Warm heat fills my head, and I know it's Tobin. He loves to run—to *chase*—but he likes to catch even more. And when he catches, he does something I can't. He fucks.

Now that I think about it, that isn't such a bad idea. If I catch her, she's dead. She's pissed me off, and I won't be able to stop myself from wrapping my hands around her throat and pressing down until she goes limp. If I let Tobin take over, she might wish for death while he's on top of her, but she'll still be alive.

And sellable.

Tobin

IT TAKES me a moment to gather my bearings as I run through the woods, but the pounding footsteps somewhere in the distance tell me everything I need to know.

She chose to run.

Kane knows he doesn't have the control to stop himself from killing her if he catches her. He also knows the catching and subsequent fucking are right up my alley. That's why he's put me in the driver's seat. That's why I'm weaving through trees and pushing past the limits of my body as I chase her down.

A sharp pain rips through my side with each breath I take. Sweat collects on my forehead and sears my eyes as it drifts past my lashes. But I don't stop. I keep running.

I catch glimpses of her in the distance, her auburn hair gripping shreds of moonlight and casting it back at me. By the way she's beginning to slow, I know she's feeling just as exhausted as I am.

"When I've finished hunting you like the filthy pig you are, I'm going to take your little cunt, do you hear me?" I let my threat wrap around her as the gap between us closes.

She lets out a shriek and stumbles into a spindly tree trunk. Her body bounces off the bark, but she doesn't stop. After a few flailing steps, she finds her feet and pushes onward. The jean skirt has ridden up her waist, giving me a peek of each pale cheek with every step she takes. Like a kick to the side, each glimpse of my prize spurs me forward.

"I can run longer than you because I want it more! Just give up now!" I yell toward her, though I don't need to yell. I'm close enough to see the way her sweat has collected on her back and darkened her shirt.

"Just let me go!"

Absolutely not.

She ducks under a low-hanging branch and cuts right. I realize what she's done too late. She's taken a path through the woods that's too narrow to accommodate my larger size. She's small enough to squeeze through the brambles and vines, but I'll get tangled if I try to follow.

I do the only thing I can and continue tracking her diagonally. I'm still in a mostly open area, so her little plan has put more distance between us, but it's also slowing her down.

I slow to a jog as she struggles through a thick patch of growth. I can hear each strangled breath from her exhausted lungs. Soon, I'll taste her fear.

"You'll wish you were dead when I finish with you! You'll wish he hadn't let me out to play!" I shout.

"He?" she screams over her shoulder. "You're such a fucking freak!"

"I'm not a freak," I say beneath ragged breaths.

She's lucky Kane isn't out to hear that word fall from her lips. He'd snap her neck for it. We've spent our whole lives being called names. Freaks. Weirdos. Anything you'd call someone you don't understand. Someone different. That word preceded Kane's first murder. That word started it all.

And once I catch her, she'll regret that word.

Chapter Ten

Aurora

My heart beats like a drum in my chest. The rhythm increases until I worry it might burst through my skin. Air sears my throat with each breath and my legs have grown weak, but I can't stop. If he catches me, I'm probably dead.

"Whore," he calls from impossibly close behind. I'm surprised he hasn't reached out and grabbed me. It's hard to ignore the urge to turn and see just how close he is, but I have to keep running. Looking behind would mean slowing down, which would mean giving him the fraction of an inch he needs to catch me.

I'm absolutely desperate to keep away from him, so I force myself to keep going. He's older than me. Surely he can't keep this up much longer.

I break through the thick growth and run into a chain-link fence on the edge of the property. The foliage camouflages it, but it gave the familiar rattle when my body careered into it. My fingers grip the metal loops as I run along the length of the fence, hoping to find an opening big enough for me but too small for him. It's too tall for me to climb, and with his muscles, he'd probably clear it with ease.

I'm so focused on finding a break in the fence that I don't realize I've come to the end of this side until I slam into the panel running the other direction. I've run out of room.

I'm cornered.

In a desperate attempt to escape him, I grip the fence and try to climb. Hand over hand, foot over foot, I grip the spaces between the metal and haul myself upward. From sheer fear and willpower, I make it to the top. Tears spring to my eyes as I hoist my leg over the top railing. I only need to get my other leg over, and then—

Firm fingers close around my ankle and rip me downward. My crotch slams onto the top of the fence, and a scream rips from me as the metal meets my pelvic bone. But there's no time to wallow in the anguish because he's pulling me back down. I send my foot into his face, and he groans, seemingly enjoying the pain I'm causing him.

"If you think I like tears, imagine how much I love blood," he growls as a trail of red trickles from his lower lip. "This is all just foreplay, eighty."

My hands bleed from clawing at the fence, which only makes it more difficult to hang on. It's like trying to grip something after smearing your palms with oil. Strength exits my body with each breath, and I have nothing left to give as he wraps his arm around my waist and pulls me to the ground.

His hands pin my arms to the cool grass. When his face nears mine, I spit in it. The moment I do, he spits back, and his blood-tinged saliva lands on my cheek.

"Stop, please!" I scream as I writhe beneath him.

He swipes the spit from his face. "I thought I was pretty fucking nice to you. You weren't hurt by what we did back in the truck, so why'd you have to go and make me chase you, huh?"

"Just let me go. I won't tell anyone. I swear."

"It's a bit late for that. I can't let you go now that I've seen how terrified you are. I drink up fear like it's liquor. Right now, you're a bottle of Everclear." He takes a deep breath before leaning over and licking the spit and blood from my cheek. "And I'm a fucking alcoholic tonight."

"I'm sorry," I say, though I don't regret trying to escape. I'm just sorry I got caught. "Just don't kill me. Please."

"Kill you? I have no plans to kill you. I had something else in mind. Will you be a good little whore and let me play, eighty?"

"Why do you keep calling me that?"

"Because it's the cost to take all of you. Mouth, pussy, ass. Whatever I want. It's how much you charge to let men like me do anything to you." He sits up, keeping his weight on my hips, and draws the money from his pocket before tossing it on my chest. The bills catch a slight breeze and try to flitter away.

If I reach for the money, I'm agreeing to let him do what he wants, and part of me wants to let the money float out of reach. A large part of me. But he'll do whatever he wants, even if I don't take the cash.

I reach for the bills, grabbing all but one of the twenties that's flown just a finger's length out of reach. He leans forward, grips the last bill, and shoves it against my chest.

"Fine," I whisper as I accept the last twenty and tuck the money into my bra.

Kane . . . Tobin—whoever it fucking is—strips off his shirt. A multitude of tattoos covers his torso. I can't make out the individual images beneath the moonlight, but I *can* see the glint of a knife as he pulls it from his waistband. My hands immediately go up, expecting him to attack me, but he lifts the blade and slices into his own chest. A soft groan vibrates his throat as he pulls the knife away from his skin, then fists my hair and pulls me up to his chest.

"Lick my blood," he growls as he pulls my face toward his skin.

My tongue touches the thin red line, and a metallic taste races over my tastebuds. He pushes the back of my head and grinds my face into his cut as if it's not enough for me to taste it. He wants to cover me with it. And he does. Warm liquid coats my face, growing sticky as it dries.

He pushes me onto my back and raises my skirt. Blood splatters on me as he leans over and pulls my underwear away from my body. Using the knife, he cuts through my panties. Warm blood drips onto my pussy, and I'd be lying if I said it doesn't feel good.

But then I feel the stiff metal blade as he grazes my slit.

Panic ratchets through me as he spreads me with one hand and puts the blade inside me with the other. It's not big, but that doesn't matter. If I move a single muscle, I'll cut myself a second vagina.

"Please get that out of me." A tear falls from the corner of my eye.

"When you're wet like you are from my blood, a small blade like this does nothing to you. It goes in and out so smoothly. But when you're dry? That's when it cuts." The blade moves in and out of me again. "As long as you stay still and don't tense up, you'll be just fine."

He fucks me with the blade, and he's much gentler than I expect him to be. Especially after that chase. But then he pulls it out of me, turns it around, and grips the blade in his powerful hand instead. He winces as it sinks into the meat of his palm, but he doesn't seem otherwise fazed.

Then he sinks the handle inside me, and all gentleness evaporates.

I'll admit, the fear and the chase have done a little something to me. The knife adds a whole different element. He sits between my legs and just pounds me with that knife as the blade slices his hand. Like a fucking psychopath, he pulls so much pleasure from the intense pain.

And like a fucking psychopath, I kind of like it, and my hips rise off the grass.

As he pulls out of me, crimson shadows his flesh. "How much of my hand can you fit inside your pretty whore cunt, huh?"

"I don't know!" I whimper. I've never had anyone put more than a few fingers inside me.

"Let's see if my blood helps grease the wheels, eighty."

His bloody fingers push inside me. Two. Then three. He draws back his arm and forces a fourth in. Warmth spreads through my core, and I accidentally moan, which he follows with a rabid groan. I'm so full, but by his estimation, I'm not full enough. He draws back, presses his thumb to his palm, and makes me take that too. He's up to his knuckles inside me, and it's almost more than I can take.

"Such a good whore. So easy to train. Spread your legs a little wider for me."

I do as he asks and part my thighs as far as they can go. He slowly twists his hand and applies firm pressure inside me. Left and right, pushing into me as he does. When he finally pushes past his knuckles, a sharp burning sensation builds around his fingers. I scream out, but once his knuckles are inside me, it feels like the worst is over. It feels like he's pushed the biggest sex toy known to man inside me. Something worthy of being a gag gift at a bachelorette party.

Something that should never actually be inside a person.

He twists his wrist, wriggling more of his hand inside me until I'm certain I can't take another millimeter. And it feels so good. Too good for something I'm being paid for. Instead of fighting the feelings, I close my eyes and lose myself to the motion of his hand inside me. Warmth works its way up my legs and runs a finger up my spine. I bear down on him as the intense pressure builds, and my come washes away the blood as he pounds me with his hand.

"Oh god!" I scream.

His eyebrows rise. "There's no god, eighty. Only me. Christen me with your come."

I have no clue what he means until he pulls out of me, leads me over to a tree, and lies down with his head against the trunk.

"Put your back against the tree for support and squat over my face," he says.

So I do. He grips my ankles and positions my feet on either side of his head, then he pushes his hand back inside me. It's a little more difficult because of the position, but he's too determined to quit. Hovering over his face with his entire hand inside me, I feel like a fucking puppet. And he's the puppet master.

I try to hold back the pressure when it builds again, but honestly, fuck this guy. I let go and squirt all over his face. My come sprays into his open mouth, and he gargles it before swallowing.

Yeah, he's a fucking freak. And not just because he thinks he's three different people.

He pulls his hand from me, unfastens his pants, and pulls out his cock. He pushes me down his body and holds me over his dick. When he pushes me down on his lap, I take him inside me.

"How do you still feel so good after having my entire fist inside you?" he growls, thrusting up to meet my core.

He grips my hair and puts the bloody, come-coated hand that was inside me in my mouth. Salt and copper tangle across my tongue. He fingers my face, and I gag until tears form at the corners of my eyes and slip down my cheeks.

"Good girl, eighty. Cry for me."

His hand pulls back enough to keep me from throwing up before he's back to fucking my throat with his fingers. Tears stream down my face as I struggle to keep from vomiting. Each time I gag, he groans when the added pressure teases his cock.

"I'll give you this. You sure know how to fuck to save your life, don't you?"

I'm not stupid. I know when to give in to a man to survive. I know how to win them over with my body. This is merely a life preserver. If I have to ride his cock for another chance to escape, then I will. Coming was just an added benefit this time.

"Thank you," I whisper.

"Fuck, you squeezing my cock like this is going to make me come."

As his hips buck against mine, I look over at the knife lying in the grass. If I just lean a little to the left—

"Don't even think about it." His grip firms on my hips and completely eliminates any chance of leaping for the knife. "I like that you considered it, though. Would you kill me as I came, whore?"

"Yes," I pant. His thrusts feel better than I wish they did.

His hips stutter against mine as he comes, probably to the thought of me stabbing him. He's such a sexual deviant, my god.

He drops his ass back to the ground. "You're a filthy girl, and I love it," he whispers, his voice all gravel. "Give my come back to me. Drip it into my mouth."

Before I can say no, he drags me up his body and positions me above his mouth again. His request doesn't even bother me, though. Dripping his come directly into his waiting mouth is nothing in the broad scheme of things.

With his hands around my thighs and his eyes closed, he sticks out his tongue and waits for my gift. I bear down, and pearly strands of come drip into his waiting mouth. I figure he'll swallow it, but he doesn't. Instead, he flips me onto my back and smirks over me.

He doesn't have to tell me what he wants me to do now.

I spread my lips, and he spits into my mouth. My come, his come, his saliva—I take all of it.

"Do you have a shred of dignity in your body, eighty? Is there anything I can't do to you?"

I swallow. I've mastered my ability to seem like I'm enjoying everything and anything because that's my job. And I'm fucking good at it. But he's also met his match. Sexual deviant, meet sexual deviant. I can only hope it will save my life in the end. Why would he want to kill a woman who would let him do anything to her?

Anything.

My gaze is drawn to the tattoo across the side of his neck. Was it Tobin who got that "daddy" tattoo? The man from the bathroom didn't seem like he'd want to be called daddy, but this man definitely seems the type. But if I'm thinking like this, does that mean I actually believe the shit he's said? That there's more than one of them? I've seen it in movies, but I didn't think it was real. Could I really be trapped in the truck with three people instead of one?

And if I am, maybe Tobin isn't the one I should be so afraid of.

Chapter Eleven

Jax

Tobin hands control to me on the walk through the woods. He's not an aftercare kind of person, and we can't let Kane out. He'll kill her for what she did. I can only hope he'll calm down before he takes control again. He knows killing her isn't the right call, not when she can fetch so much money from The Nameless. But Kane also has very weak-impulse control. We can only hold him back for so long, though.

We reach the truck, and I beeline for the sink as soon as we're inside. Blood stains my shirt, my face, my hands, and because it's drying, it's a sticky mess. Using a stiff rag draped over the side of the sink, I begin to scrub.

Tobin loves blood, but it's not a shared interest. I can't wait to get it off my hands. I rub until every inch of my exposed skin is raw and red, being careful around the new cut Tobin has put on our body. It's not very deep, but it still doesn't feel great when the rag's tough fibers scrape across it.

"You really aren't Tobin, are you?" she asks as I continue my furious scrubbing.

I glance at her in the mirror. She's seated on the bed, wringing her scraped hands in front of her. "I tried to tell you that. I'm really not Tobin."

"And you aren't Kane."

"I'm none of them. I'm me. Jax."

"But Kane's the boss?"

I shake my head. "Not exactly. Kane is the main. He's the one who was born in that physical body."

"But you guys are your own people?"

I dry my face with a paper towel. "Yes, we're different personality states sharing one body. We have our own strengths and weaknesses, likes and dislikes."

"And do *you* like holding women captive, Jax?" she asks.

"Of course not. I don't like anything about this situation. But Kane does, and I have an obligation to him. It's nothing against you. We just have to protect ourselves."

I wipe my hand down my face, and my gaze falls on her hands again. Some of the gouges on her palms look pretty filthy. They need to be cleaned and tended, and Kane and Tobin sure as fuck won't bother with it.

I motion her over to the sink. "Wash your hands. You don't want those cuts to get infected."

She stands on shaky legs and approaches the sink, keeping her eyes on me the entire time. She still doubts what I've said, and how she doesn't believe there are three of us is beyond me. We couldn't be more different. Even when we're boiled down to our base desires, we're nothing alike. If I fuck, it's soft and sweet. If Tobin fucks, it's that bloody mess swirling down the drain. And Kane won't fuck at all.

Now that her hands are cleaned of blood, I can see that

the cuts aren't too bad after all, which is good because we don't exactly keep a first-aid kit in the truck. Kane isn't in the business of healing wounds. He'd rather create them. I don't know what she'll do about the bloodstains between her legs, though. For tonight, I just have to make sure she's tucked away in bed so we can actually get some rest. Sleep deprivation isn't great for any of us.

Aurora doesn't need help figuring out how to get clean, though. She rinses the rag I used, lifts her skirt, and begins scrubbing between her legs. I turn away.

"You can look, Jax," she whispers.

Instead of responding, I head toward the front of the truck and plop down in the seat. She's trying to bait me, but I can't fall into her trap. As I flip the hat around and lower it over my eyes, I focus on my need for a shower. I want nothing more than to clean the blood from my junk, and that's something I can't do until I figure out where Kane keeps the restraints.

I have to make sure she can't run off. Because she will. The first time the opportunity presents itself, she'll take off again.

The water is still running, so I'm a bit shocked when her hand grazes my shoulder. She walks between the seats and sits on my lap. Her warmth burns me, but I don't shove her away. Instead, I take the time to look at her. Her appearance was the reason I began staring at her in the first place.

She licks her full lips, and I'm tempted to lean forward and kiss her. It's been a long time since I've felt a woman's caress, but I've never been with a woman as stunning as Aurora. Even though she looks a little tired, a little beaten down from what she's been through at our hands, she's still beautiful.

Aurora turns and straddles my lap. Her hand goes for my cheek as she leans in, but I turn away.

"We can't," I say. I speak as firmly as I can muster, but my voice sounds weak to my ears. I don't get to play like this very often. Tobin comes knocking at any chance of sex, and I'm cast aside because my personality isn't as strong as his. But Tobin is spent, and my mind is silent for once.

"There's no one here but us, Jax. Sure we can."

I'm not an idiot. She's only trying to win me over so she can escape. She doesn't actually like me. But someone needs to tell my dick this revelation.

My pierced, tattooed dick.

My god. I look like an idiot with this thing. I think it's trashy, but then I remember who orchestrated the entire thing. Tobin. Need I say more?

"I know what you're trying to do. You're trying to lower my defenses so you can escape again," I say.

She shakes her head and looks away. "I know that's useless now. I can't run from you. But I want to see if it's different when I fuck you."

Oh, it would be very different. For starters, I won't draw any blood.

Even though I know it's a ploy, she tears down my defenses when her eyes meet mine again. When her hands move toward my lap, I don't stop her. When she unzips my pants and reveals my fully erect cock, I allow it.

My eyes remain on hers as she rises and lowers herself onto me. Her warmth envelops me, and I groan and rest the back of my head against the leather seat. I revel in the way she grips my cock with each movement of her hips and thighs. Her breasts bounce slightly with each up-and-down motion, and I long to take them into my mouth. I long to taste her.

I put my hand behind her neck, draw her into me, and kiss her. She returns the kiss, meeting each surge of my tongue with hers. I raise my hips and meet her next motion halfway, thrusting my full length into her, and she moans into my mouth.

She pulls back and continues rocking on my lap. "When was the last time you fucked?"

"Years. Five maybe," I pant against her neck.

"They don't let you out to play?"

"Not like this." I reach around her waist and grip the steering wheel as she fucks me.

"How does it feel?" she whispers.

"So fucking good."

She increases the speed, riding me harder, and if I don't change positions, I'll come too soon. How fucking ridiculous.

"Let's take this to the bed," I say, and she nods.

I ease her off my lap and guide her toward the back of the truck. I don't even care about the blood on us as I lay her down and get between her legs. I only want to feel her again.

I wrap her thighs around me as I push inside her. She looks up at me with those pretty green eyes as her moans drift from her lips, and I fuck her a little harder so I can draw more of that out of her. Tobin already filled her, but I can't be mad about another man's come. Not when I have this perfect woman beneath me. Instead of focusing on the warm stickiness as I thrust into her, I focus on the soft moan she releases or the way her body responds to mine.

My hand moves between us, and I rub tight circles around her clit. When she clenches around me, I know I'm in the right spot.

Or am I? She's a professional at this, and there's a lot more at stake than a stack of cash this time.

"Don't fake it for me, sweet girl. I can always tell," I say.

"I'm not faking anything," she says. "I'm going to come."

If she's really that close, I want her to come on my tongue. I pull out and kneel at the edge of the bed. Gripping her thighs, I pull her toward my face, only taking a moment to admire the beautiful pussy in front of me. Aside from the bloody smears, it's perfection.

Now I need to know if it's as delicious as it looks.

I hook my arms around her thighs and bring my mouth to her slit. I lick, tasting everything from tonight. It's not great, but her taste lies beneath it all. Warm and sweet. I focus on that as I tongue her.

As I gently suck her swollen clit, her moans shift. They're less restrained. Her fingers clutch the sheets, and her hips begin to move. She chases each stroke of my tongue as her thighs begin to quiver in my grasp.

"Holy fuck," she pants.

I push my fingers inside her, and she gasps as she draws closer to her edge. Her breath comes in sharp bursts, matching each flick of my tongue as I tease her and give her a little push. I want her to fall over that edge. I want to taste every drop of her genuine pleasure.

"I'm going to come!" she screams.

"Who's making you come?" I ask.

"Jax," she moans.

Hearing my name fall from her parted lips sends an ache right to the hardened flesh between my legs. She tightens around my fingers, and warm wetness overflows from her. I lean down and scoop up every drop with my tongue. I don't care that Tobin's pleasure has mixed with hers. I don't care that the metallic tang of blood permeates her sweet flavor. I want to drink her like wine, and nothing will stop me from curling my tongue along her clit as her body shudders.

As she begins to come down from her orgasm, I fist my cock and push inside her again. Firm, pleasure-filled spasms squeeze me again and again. I've never felt something so incredible. It's as if my body was made for hers.

I reach forward and grip her breast in my hand. The hard point presses against my palm as she pushes her chest upward. My hand travels down her stomach, reveling in each panting breath she takes. It's too much. I can't hold back any longer.

I pull out of her and stroke myself. Instead of coming inside her, I want to watch my come paint her pretty little pussy. As I feel the pressure build, I squeeze just beneath the base of my cock and send come spurting onto her skin. I empty everything onto her, then I draw my hips back and push inside her again. I'm sensitive after I come, but it's a reminder that I was given the gift of release as my head strokes her walls again.

When I can't take it anymore, I pull out and lie beside her. My hand rubs between her legs, smearing my come into her skin. God, she's incredible. She's—

"You could let me go, Jax," she whispers.

My hand stops moving. As does my heart. I knew this was all part of her game, but I let myself forget for just a moment. I didn't want to think about it, but now she's forcing me to.

"Aurora, you know I can't."

"If you don't let me go, Kane or Tobin will kill me."

I shake my head. "Tobin wouldn't."

She doesn't respond. How can she? We both know what we're up against. We both know I can't say that Kane wouldn't kill her. He would. Even with the plan to give her to The Nameless, he still might.

"I can't let you go. You don't understand how this works."

"So explain it to me. Help me understand."

I'd almost rather let her go than try to explain our situation to her. To explain what it means to be three minds in one body. I've seen the looks before. People either think it's all an act or that we're crazy. Sometimes both. But no one truly understands because no one ever *tries* to understand. They would rather fear and ostracize the unknown than take the time to hear it out.

Considering letting her go only pisses Kane off. I feel him in my mind, lurking just behind a door that he can easily break down. But this girl doesn't get it. How can I make her understand?

I suck in a deep breath. "Fine. You can go."

Fire blazes against the backs of my eyes, and a headache knocks against my skull. I stay on the bed as she rushes to find her backpack. She looks back at me for help, but I can only shrug my shoulders and rub my burning eyes. I don't know where Kane hid it. She finally gives up and heads for the door.

And just as she opens it, the door holding back Kane swings wide.

Chapter Twelve

Kane

These fucking idiots. This is why sex isn't even a thought in my mind. It makes you fucking stupid. With my pants still undone, I run after her. She isn't hard to find. Instead of racing for the woods, I catch a glimpse of her shirt as she bolts toward the bathrooms.

Too slow, dropout.

She's caught off guard as I catch up to her and yank her back by the hair. A scream tears from her chest as her leg lashes toward me, but I have a solution for that. I grab her legs and take out her feet. Her head collides with the grass, and the screaming stops.

Knocking her out wasn't the goal—The Nameless don't like girls with bruises—but she left me no fucking choice. The rest area is empty now, but someone could drive up at any moment. If someone hears her screaming and sees me chasing her and hauling her back to my truck, it's a guaranteed one-way trip to the nearest jail cell. Even if Tobin doesn't give a shit, Jax sure as fuck does. I can't believe he let her go.

I kneel beside her still form and get my arms under her. Getting her to the truck before someone drives by is my first priority. I can check the goods for damage once we're safely inside.

I climb the metal steps and enter the truck with her limp body in my arms. Once we're tucked away from prying eyes, I drop the caring-guy act and drag her toward the bed by her hair. I pull a scuffed set of handcuffs from the cabinet above the bed, then attach one cuff to her arm and the other to the metal hinge connected to my bed.

She isn't going anywhere now.

I grip her face and turn it toward me. A large red welt puffs her cheek outward, but it doesn't look like it will bruise. Or if it does, it won't be too bad. This almost pisses me off more than if she'd been seriously injured. My hands itch with the need to wrap my fingers around her pale neck. She's a pain in my ass, and I'll be glad when I get rid of her.

I'm about to walk away when I notice the mess between her legs. Her skirt has ridden up, exposing her filthy pussy. I grab a few paper towels and begin cleaning her up. With each not-so-tender swipe, my lip curls further.

I have no clue what those boneheads find so appealing about her pussy. I couldn't be more turned off by the used-up slit between her legs. Something inside me heats to a boil when I stare at those puffy folds of skin. A memory thrashes within a locked box inside my head, fighting to break free, and I can't have that. I need to do something, and fast.

I grab a lighter from my pocket, spread her lips, and flick the metal until a flame springs forth. I bring the heat toward the swollen bundle of nerves that brings her so much dirty pleasure. I should burn that sinful clit off. Maybe Jax and Tobin won't be so interested in her if I damage her a little.

As I stare down at her pussy, memories seep from the locked box like invisible gas.

Big, feminine hands reach for my lap. I'm crying. She pulls me onto her naked thighs . . .

Anger roars like a lion inside me. I don't know who that was, but I know it's a woman. She's the reason I hate women now, and I don't need to know from what well that hatred springs. I know that it's poisoned, filthy and black, and I drink from it daily. The source isn't important as long as the water keeps flowing.

I drop the lighter and clench my eyes shut. I don't want to remember. I don't want to know what happened to me. Tobin spoon-feeds little glimpses from time to time, but I don't want that right now.

I lower the girl's skirt and scoot away from her. I need to sell her, so her body isn't mine to permanently damage. If I wasn't giving her to The Nameless, I'd cut off her clit and feed it to her for running away. Twice.

But that isn't a solution.

Maybe I should cut off my own dick to stop Tobin and Jax from using it and becoming complete dumb asses.

I bring the lighter up to my limp cock and flick the metal again. Heat bursts from the opening, and I revel in the flames licking my sensitive skin. The scent of burned flesh wafts up to me, and I release the lighter. I was so lost in the pleasurable pain that I didn't realize I nearly gave myself a second-degree burn. The thought of how the pain would zip straight to my brain if I'd done more damage tempts me to continue, but I don't. I stuff the lighter into my pocket and turn my attention back to the problem at hand.

The girl.

Killing or maiming her would make her less desirable to Jax and Tobin, but it would do me no good. Aside from the fleeting thrill of a kill, I'd get nothing out of it. I have to find a way to remind the others that she doesn't belong to us. She isn't ours to catch and release at will. She's a commodity.

I go to the front of my truck and pull the burner phone from the concealed compartment beneath my seat. After tapping in the number—it's too risky to save it as a contact—I hit the call button. One of The Nameless answers on the second ring.

"Talk."

"I'm hauling a load your way," I say. "Should I come to the usual spot, or—"

"No. Contact me when you reach Houston. I'll give you an address. Where are you coming from?"

I glance at the brick building, then back at the interstate. Headlights push through the trees as someone pulls into the parking lot. "I'm in Ohio right now. Shouldn't take too long to get there."

"Give me the details so I can line up a buyer. We aren't in a position to hold the product for very long right now. Better to move them quickly."

I smirk. I know what sort of men will be buying this product, and it's exactly what she deserves. I give him the code for a pretty redhead, no apparent drug habits, clean and clear.

"I'm not taking it if the packaging is damaged," he says. "I cut you a break last time. Never again."

My eyes close, and I nod as I end the call. It's a warning I must heed, and now that The Nameless have been promised something, it's a warning Jax and Tobin are forced to heed as well.

I zip my pants and return to the cabinet above the bed.

After digging around inside, I find the choke collar and metal leash, and I drop them on the counter beside the sink. The girl is too unruly. If she wants to act like a dog and run away at every opportunity, I'll treat her like one. The next time we leave this truck, I plan to keep her on a very short leash.

Chapter Thirteen

Aurora

I blink back my confusion. The hum of tires on asphalt vibrates the truck. We're moving, then. Swimming up from the blackness, I'm left with a headache and a lot of questions. My eyes rise to the small, dirty window. A pale orange glow filters through, telling me the sun has just begun to rise.

I've survived my first night with Kane. Or Jax. Or Tobin. Whoever he's pretending to be today. I'm still not sure I believe him.

When I try to sit up, metal rattles. A handcuff winds around my wrist, securing me to the bed. Memories rush back to me. I remember sleeping with Jax, and then he let me go. I guess Kane didn't agree with that. I growl as I try to free my hand from the shining metal bracelet, but there's no give.

Fucking fuck.

Pup stirs beside me. Her fluffy paws push forward as she stretches, and she opens her mouth in a yawn. I reach out and give her a soothing pat with my free hand. Her brown eyes close again.

I collapse on the bed. My bladder aches, and I can smell myself. I need a shower and a bathroom break.

"Kane!" I yell, but he doesn't answer.

I have to find a way out of this shitty situation I'm in, and escape is my only option. Even though every attempt has failed thus far, I can't give up. I won't die in this fucking truck.

It feels like forever before the truck stops moving. The curtain whips open and his menacing face glares at me. He looks like he's still sick and tired of my shit. Well, I'm sick and tired of his shit, too.

"What, dropout?"

"I have to pee."

He turns to leave.

"And shower!"

Metal rattles, and he shows up again . . . with a chain in his hand. It looks like a collar and leash. Pup raises her head and wags her tail. How she looks at him with such adoration in her big brown eyes is beyond me.

"Really?" I say.

"If you want to act like a dog that's hell-bent on escaping its yard, you'll be treated like one." He moves closer and clasps the collar around my neck, then rips the leash backward. The metal comes together and pinches my skin between the links, and I whimper. "Are you going to behave yourself?"

It's not as if he's given me a choice. "Yes."

He unlocks the handcuff, and I rub the red indentations on my wrist. My entire body aches from all the running and fucking I've done in the past twenty-four hours, but I can only focus on the relief my hand feels at being free again.

"I need to wash my clothes," I say. "I have a few outfits in my backpack, but they're all dirty. And I don't know what you did with my bag."

Instead of responding, he drops the leash and goes toward a row of cabinets. They open and close as he pulls women's clothes from inside. He tucks some under his arm, grips the leash once again, and drags me forward. Do I even want to know why he has women's clothes in here? How many girls came before me?

He catches me staring. "They're from women who didn't need them anymore."

"Did you kill them?"

"What did I say about asking questions? Best you don't."

"Are you going to kill me?"

Instead of answering, he just turns around and pulls the leash. I take a quick step forward, not wanting to feel the collar's bite again.

We get off the truck and I blink against the growing sunlight. We're at a different rest stop, but this one isn't nearly as clean as the last one. Kane drags me toward the building. There's no one else around, and I'm partly grateful no one else can witness this humiliation. Another part of me wouldn't mind if someone saw because it would mean I could yell for help.

But would I yell for help if given the chance?

I don't know.

This guy—or this particular personality, if he's telling the truth—is completely unhinged. If I yell for help, I'm potentially dragging someone else into the danger zone. That's not something I can live with. Then again, I would need to be alive to feel bad about it later.

Kane snatches the leash, dragging me out of my

thoughts with a sharp, pain-filled reminder. I hurry and follow him before he can do it again.

Once we're inside the bathroom, he turns to me. "On the ground. Dogs walk on all fours."

I bite my lip as I look at the years of filth coating the floor. The sticky mess clutching the bottoms of my shoes goes beyond mud and mildew. And the smells. It's like the people who used this restroom chose to piss everywhere but in the urinals.

His grip tightens on the leash.

Fuck, I don't want to do this, but he's looking at me like I have no choice.

When I don't move, he wraps the leash around his hand and raises it high above my head. The pain comes first. Instead of a sharp pinch like before, the metal catches the skin at the back of my neck and squeezes it between the links, holding it there. I reach behind my head and try to relieve the tension, but it's no use.

Then I realize the real danger. He's strangling me.

I push my fingers against the collar, trying to give myself room to draw a breath, but there's no space between the thick circles and my skin. My feet begin to rise from the floor, and crawling through the filth doesn't seem so bad now. Stars dance in front of my eyes, and a black curtain begins to close around the edge of my vision.

I nod my head, hoping he'll understand the meaning. I'll do what he wants.

He releases the leash, and I fall to my hands and knees, forcing back a gag as I land in a wet spot. I gasp for air, each breath coated in the scent of stale urine and mold.

"I can't kill you, so I'm going to enjoy myself by degrading the fuck out of you. Do you understand?"

"Why?" I ask, my throat still tight. The single word sends me into a coughing fit.

"Because I fucking *hate* women. Jax and Tobin may be able to have sex with you, but my cock shrivels at the sight of disgusting fucking whores like you."

I swallow hard. Tell me how you really feel, dude.

The ice in his words makes me more certain they aren't the same people at all. Jax, Tobin, and Kane are just too different. Even if I can't understand it, I'm forced to believe it. If he were acting, he'd have broken character at some point.

He pulls me toward the urinal, and I crawl behind him. "Sit," he commands.

I do as I'm told, and the cuffs of my ass rub on the ground as my skirt rides up. I try to lower the stiff fabric, but it's no use.

"Put your head beside the urinal and open your fucking mouth," he says.

I already know where this is going before he unzips his pants, and I don't like it. He wiggles the leash in his hand. A warning. I lick my lips before parting them, and my stomach threatens to cast up everything I've ever eaten.

"Now close your eyes," he says, and I do.

Seconds pass like hours as I sit on the disgusting floor and wait for this man to piss in my mouth. I mentally prepare myself for the salty bite and the acrid perfume of someone else's waste, but how does someone prepare for something like this?

The anticipation is probably worse than the actual act.

I hear the splash of urine before I feel it, but thankfully, I only feel the droplets ricocheting from the urinal and landing on my shoulder. Disgusting, but far better than the alternative. He finishes pissing, shakes it off, and puts it away. I hear this instead of seeing it because my eyes are still closed. I don't dare open them now. I'm starting to figure him out. He likes to play a mental game as well as a physical one.

"Open your eyes, dropout."

I do, and I'm relieved to see his hand reaching for the flush lever instead of the leash. But then he stops.

"No, you know what? Flush it for me."

I reach for the lever above my head, but he rips my hand away and yanks me to my knees.

"Not like that. I want you to use your filthy mouth. Now."

Oh Jesus. No. I imagine the ghosts of every man's filthy hand on the metal lever. Hands that have just touched their junk. Hands that might have scratched an itchy butthole. Hands that have been in numerous dirty places I can't even conjure in my mind. And he wants me to put my mouth on it.

His other hand buries itself in my hair before he forces my face toward the rusted metal lever. He rubs my cheek against it before drawing back my head and placing my pinched lips right on the tip. Maybe it won't be so bad. I can just use my teeth to—

"Suck it."

The color drains from my face, and I lose feeling in my limbs. It's bad enough that he wants me to use my mouth to flush the fucking urinal, but now he wants me to fellate it as well? I glance at him, hoping he's just testing me the way he did moments ago, but his eyes hold no humor. He's serious.

Having no other choice, I spread my lips and take the lever into my mouth. I puff air in and out of my throat, refusing to breathe through my nose. If I have to smell whatever lives on this lever—coupled with the grimy feel of the handle—I'll puke.

"Stop cheating," he says. "Close those lips around it and show me what you can do."

Fuck.

Like the dog I am, I obey. My lips form a seal around the metal rod, and I give the urinal the best blow job it's ever had. I suck and lick until I've worn off at least one coat of rust, but it's still not enough for him. He grips the back of my head and forces the whole thing into my mouth. He fucks my face with it, and I can no longer stop my stomach from clenching. As I gag, my back teeth scrape against the metal, sending a bolt of pain into my skull.

Having had enough fun, he cranes my neck so that my front teeth grip the metal, then he pulls my head down until the urinal flushes. He rips my head away and turns me toward him, his lips only inches from mine.

"I hope that pissy flusher tastes terrible, whore."

"It does," I pant, fighting back the gags wrenching my stomach in an iron fist.

I hate that it doesn't make me vomit. It should. But one time I got paid two hundred dollars to tongue a public toilet seat as a client fucked me from behind. He even slammed my head beneath the thing and put me beneath the water. Yes, I agreed to it. Yes, I hated it. But money is a fierce motivator when you have nothing but your body to give away.

Now I'm performing for something more meaningful than money. I'm performing for my life.

Chapter Fourteen

Kane

Tobin left a note for me. In it, he said the girl is unbreakable, and that only made me want to break her more. When I say I want to break her, I mean in the most final kind of way, but that isn't possible. Especially not now that I've promised her to The Nameless. So I've challenged myself to break her emotionally instead of physically. She's fucking steadfast, I'll give her that. She hasn't shed a single tear during all of this.

And I want her to cry for me.

Unlike Tobin, I don't want tears of shame. I want tears of devastation and destruction. I want tears from heartbreak and hopelessness. I want to lap the proof of her pain from her cheeks.

This girl, though . . . She's proving to be a steel-skinned enigma. Every other woman I've taken would be a begging, blubbering mess by now, annoying the fuck out of me with their pleading. That's half the reason I finally get rid of them. I get sick of the noise.

I will break her eventually. Women are fucking weak. They're an inferior species. Emotionally driven. Physically limited. She might be a tougher nut to crack, but it doesn't mean she's uncrackable.

"You want to clean up?" I ask.

She nods. She probably sees this as a kindness on my part. It's not. When people are scared, their sweat smells different. Worse. That smell triggers something in my brain and agitates what lies in the locked box. I know I smelled like that once, but I don't know why. I only know that I don't want to smell it right now.

Usually I get rid of the stink by dumping it a few feet below ground, but I'm stuck with this girl until I hand her off. I'm allowing her to clean herself for *my* sake.

"Get undressed," I say.

She pulls her shirt over her head and hands it to me so I can feed the leash through the shirt's collar. With that done, I attach the leash to the top of the stall wall. She doesn't have much room to move without tightening the collar around her neck, which is perfect. Maybe she'll slip and hang herself. A man can dream.

After removing her bra and skirt, she stands and shivers in front of me. I love it. I'm also a bit frustrated by it. She's pretty. Nice curves. My eyes drop to her tits, pressed together by her arms as she tries to cover herself. I see why Jax and Tobin are so attracted to her, but the disconnect in my brain doesn't allow that attraction to reach my groin. It's like a theater of people crying at the end of a movie while I sit there and twiddle my fucking thumbs. I know why they're upset, but I feel nothing.

She eyes me as I strip off my clothes and step up to the sink. Using a rag I tucked inside the bundle of clothes, I gather a bit of soap from the dispenser and begin washing my body. This isn't the first time I've taken a whore's bath, and years on the road have taught me how to be quick. Once I've used another wet rag to rinse the soap from my body, I don't dress. I stay naked because her gaze keeps flicking toward my dick as she shifts her weight between her feet. She's uncomfortable, which is just how I want her to feel.

I release the chain a bit so she can move toward the sink, but she has to strain and contort her body to alleviate the pressure on her neck. She cleans off the best she can, her breath coming out in strained gasps as the chain tightens around her throat with every motion. Again, she says nothing. Just takes it all in stride.

And it pisses me off.

I consider foregoing my meeting with The Nameless. Having my debt knocked down would be great, but breaking this girl would be even better. Even a stoic bitch like her would cry for me before I string her intestines around my truck like fucking Christmas lights. Or maybe I could grind the skin from her fucking face with a sander. That thought almost makes me hard.

I release the leash when she's finished cleaning the stink from her skin, then I drag her to the mirror. Grime and fingerprints mar her reflection. I fist her hair, crane her neck, and make her look at herself.

"No matter how much you clean yourself, you're still filthy," I say. "Never forget that."

I expect her to close her eyes or show some sign of shame, but yet again, she's fearless in the face of depravity. My brain pings with ideas as I consider other ways to break her before I have to hand her off. I can't do anything that would leave a lasting mark, which completely rules out cutting and beating. Two of my favorite things.

Choking her is fun, but I'm liable to go too far if I keep on.

When I look at her throat again, a light bulb blazes above my head. A few months ago, Tobin bought an industrial-strength shock collar for Pup. I was able to break through and hide it before he could use it on my dog, but now I think I've found a good use for it. He never had the chance to cut the collar to size, so it should be big enough to go around Aurora's neck. It's rated for disobedient creatures with a high pain tolerance, and that pretty much describes the girl.

With a new plan in mind, I help to dress her in black leggings and a dress shirt a previous victim left behind. It's not like she'll need the clothes anymore. The girl looks pretty when she's dressed up like this, and I like pretty things.

I love to kill them once I've dolled them up. When they look their best and feel their worst. I don't need to slather this girl with makeup to make her look nice, though. She only needed to be washed and dressed in something that wasn't so slutty.

Killing is the closest I come to feeling something, and thoughts of spilling blood on that dress shirt almost harden me. Her fear would be my foreplay, and killing her would be the main event. Murder grants the release I crave, but I can't do any of that, so I'll have to make do with torture. With a smile on my face, I lead her back to the truck.

Chapter Fifteen

Aurora

Once we're back in the truck, he removes the collar and leash and hooks me to the bed again. The handcuff digs into my wrist. As I sit here, held captive in a madman's truck, I'm just glad I'm clean. Such a treasured luxury for someone like me. I rub my free hand along my neck, feeling the indents and bruising where he choked me with the collar. Dick.

Psychos like it when you freak out and react to their madness. He'll be sorely disappointed in me. It would take a lot to make me react to him. I'm used to degradation and pain. What I'm not used to is the lack of payment afterward. *That* pisses me off.

My arm strains as I lean over to look at him. His body sways as he pulls things from compartments near the front of the truck. I don't know what he's looking for, and I'm not sure I want to know. I turn my attention to that tiny window again.

Sitting up on my knees and straining my neck, I can

make out the sign near the front of the rest stop. A sign that sends my heart to my feet. He's taken us south, not north. We're already in fucking Kentucky! It was stupid of me to think he'd bring me home after all this, but seeing the sign hits me with a hard truth.

"Where are you taking me?" I yell. The chain rattles on my wrist.

"I have business to do."

"Where?"

"South."

I take a sharp breath. "Kane, just let me go. You haven't done anything to me that would make me go to the police. No harm, no foul. We can just go our own way." I try to keep my voice calm and steady so he knows I'm serious. If he lets me go, I won't go to the police. They don't believe whores anyway.

"Shut up, dropout," he says as his back straightens. He holds a box in his hand, and I don't want to find out what waits inside.

"I'm serious. You're safe. The cops wouldn't believe me, even if I ran to them." I don't add that I'm speaking from firsthand experience.

"I've never been safe in my entire life," he says. "And now, neither are you."

"You think I've been safe? People who've known safety don't take all the things you guys have done to me on the fucking chin."

Kane lifts his bandaged hand and examines it. "How did this happen?"

"You . . . Tobin cut his hand when he was fucking me with the handle of a knife."

Kane scoffs. "And you liked it?"

"Maybe not that part, but if you're asking if I came with

his entire hand inside me while he used his blood as lubrication? Yeah. That happened."

He shakes his head and comes toward me, the box still clutched in his hand. Panic sends bile into my throat, but I keep still. He pulls something black from the box and steps closer. I can't see what it is.

"Close your eyes," he says. It's the sort of thing you'd expect someone to say with a smile, but he's as serious as a terminal diagnosis.

Most people wouldn't obey him, but I'm beginning to learn his personalities. This one has a short fuse. If I don't want to set him off, I should close my fucking eyes.

So I do.

Something wraps around my throat, and I fight the urge to fling my hand toward my neck and pull it away. Pup licks my hand. I stroke her fur to calm myself while a storm rages in my mind, thundering for me to scream and fight him off. Then he steps away and takes whatever he put around my neck with him.

"Don't open your eyes, dropout."

It's true, what they say. When you're deprived of a sense, your others are heightened. I can't see what he's doing, but I can hear it. He pulls out a drawer, and the wheels squeak. Metal *shicks* against metal as he cuts something with scissors. Whatever he's cut away falls to the floor, landing in an almost imperceptible whisper. Footsteps thud toward me. Warm breath whispers through my hair as his hands position something around my neck.

And this time, I know what it is.

My eyes pop open.

Zap!

My body jerks from the surprise, but it doesn't hurt that bad.

"I didn't say you could open them yet," he says. He zaps me again, but I don't jerk this time. He'll have to try harder if he wants another reaction.

"What's the point of this?" I ask.

As I reach for the shock collar around my throat, he fiddles with something on the remote in his hand.

Zap! Zap!

"Fuck!" I can't hold back the expletive this time. That fucking hurt. "Did you plan to use this on your tiny dog? It's made for something with a much higher—"

Zap!

My mouth slams shut. Is a tool like this even legal?

When I look at him again, he no longer wears the hardened face of the man who handcuffed me to the bed. His expression is soft and sweet. Handsome. He's another person entirely. And when my eyes travel down his body and stop at his erection, I know he's no longer Kane.

"Sorry you're chained," he says.

"Are you going to release me?" I ask.

"No fucking way. You're already chained for me. You tried to escape again, didn't you? Such a bad little whore."

It's Tobin. The sexual alter. I can make this work in my favor.

He steps closer and fingers the collar around my neck. "Hey, I bought that for Pup. I guess Kane found a better use for it. But how did you get these marks on your neck, eighty? The shock collar wouldn't do that."

I swallow against the pulse in his fingertips. "He used another collar. A choke chain. If I wanted to bathe myself, I had to lean against it."

"And you just kept leaning into that pressure? What a sadistic slut."

"You do what you have to do," I whisper.

"You sure do, don't you? Shove a bottle in your cunt. Take a whole fist inside you. Hang like a guilty whore." His hand tightens around the shock collar.

Tobin is a sexual sadist, but I can't deny my attraction to him. Even Kane is attractive with that face, but as Tobin, the attraction multiplies. He's rough and completely unhinged. At this point, I'm giving him things I'd charge others extra for. Not that he'd pay anyway.

And why shouldn't I get a little enjoyment out of this? If I'm doomed to die at his hands, I might as well enjoy a few orgasms from those same hands as well.

"Let's play a little game," he says through a smile. "I'm going to do whatever I want to your body, and you're going to stay completely silent. Each time you make a sound . . ." He wiggles the remote in his hand.

This doesn't sound like a very fun game. Maybe if he turns it down a few notches, I could enjoy it more. I open my mouth to say as much, but his finger depresses the button before I can speak. A dizzying jolt shoots through my neck, tensing the muscles.

"It wasn't a question, and the game has already started," he says. "Better keep quiet."

He pulls off his pants and climbs on top of me, resting his cock against me. Warmth and strength press against the leggings, and I want them off. I wiggle my legs without making a sound.

"Oh, you want these off?" he says. "You should ask me to remove them."

I look up at him, pleading with my eyes, but he only raises his eyebrows. My lips part, but the sound won't come. Is it worth the impending shock?

"I want you to take them—"

The zap cuts off my voice, but it's a small price to pay

for the sweet relief of feeling his hands working the fabric away from my body. When I'm bare, he looks between my legs and licks his lips.

"Spread wider. I want to see your dirty pussy."

And god, why do those cruel words send a jolt of pleasure to my core? I part my knees for him, and he swipes a finger through my slit. Pleasure singes my nerve endings before he pulls his touch away.

"You're so wet. Tell me why, eighty."

I shake my head, and his fingers shoot toward my scalp. He winds his hand through my hair, twisting until he has a good grip. Then he snatches back my head and bends closer to my mouth.

His lips move over mine as he speaks again. "Tell me why you're so wet. Don't be shy."

"You made me th—"

He presses the button, and my throat tightens into a whimper. That earns me another shock, but I don't make a sound this time. After releasing my hair, he gives my cheek a light slap.

"Such a good little whore. I like playing with you." A low growl follows his words as he raises my shirt and reaches for my nipple. At first he's gentle, tweaking the tight nub between his fingers. He lowers his mouth to my breast, laving the skin with the flat of his tongue before using his teeth to put pressure on the most sensitive place.

I cry out. It's partly from pleasure and partly from pain, but none of that matters because I've made a sound. He shocks me again.

"Don't be naughty," he whispers against my skin. "I *hate* having to punish you, but you keep forcing my hand."

Sarcasm drips from his voice. He hates none of this. He lives for it. And right now, so do I.

Since I can't speak, I push my chest against his mouth again, begging for more. He cups my breast with his hand and closes his mouth over my nipple, but I'm ready this time. When he bites down, I grit my teeth and allow myself to feel it. The ache. The ecstasy. It melds into one mind-blowing sensation and travels down my spine.

His hand moves to the warm space between my legs, pressing tight circles around my clit as he alternates between teasing and biting my skin. Pleasure-filled whimpers climb my throat, but I swallow each one.

"Fuck, you're so wet. Are you ready for me?" he asks.

I nod my head.

"Tell me."

I open my mouth, but before I can utter a sound, the numbing zap tears across my skin. This game is impossible to win, but I don't mind. Each time I lose, I'm brought closer to my edge.

His hips draw back, and he thrusts inside me. I hold each whimper and moan, refusing to let them out, but I don't know how long I can keep this up. He feels so good inside me. With each thrust, the head of his cock pushes me closer as his girth fills me completely. That barbell is the metal cherry on top.

"This won't do," he says in answer to my silence. His hand goes to the collar, and he unfastens it from my neck. His fingers replace the collar, and he continues thrusting.

As I let out a whimper, his grip tightens. This isn't just playful breath play. I can't draw any air, and he shows no signs of letting up. His thrusts quicken to a hammering tempo, fucking me harder than I've ever been fucked. I'm sucked into a dizzying wave of euphoria, but I'm fading too fast. My vision blackens as my mouth gapes, and I lose consciousness.

When I wake up, he's still fucking me. His grip has moved away from my throat, and something cold presses against my clit.

"Welcome back, eighty," he whispers. "You feel so good, but I know what will make you feel better."

Zzzt!

Lightning shoots through my clit, simultaneously numbing it and leaving it overly sensitive. My pussy reacts by clamping around him and sending an ache through my core. He groans and fucks me harder.

"Again," I whisper.

Why did I fucking like it? Why does this sadistic act bring me so much pleasure? But the answers don't matter as he smiles and looks down at me.

"Again? What's wrong with you?" He laughs. "Actually, what's so fucking *right* with you?"

He presses the button again, and my pussy convulses around him. I cry out, unable to keep quiet with so much happening inside my body. I'm so close, and I want to come.

He leans down and hovers above me with his mouth so close to mine. I want to lean up and kiss him, but something about him tells me he isn't the kissing type.

"Fucking kiss me," I rasp.

"I don't kiss whores."

"Then punish me until I come."

A sinful smirk crosses his lips, and he sits up. He places the shock collar remote in my hand, giving me control of one form of punishment. Holding the collar to my pussy with one hand, his other hand moves to my throat, slowly cutting off my breath.

"Are you going to die for me, whore?" he growls.

I press the button as another wave of darkness closes in. Invisible sparks shoot through my clit, tightening the bundle of nerves, but I lose consciousness just as I feel my orgasm building. When I come to, he's looking down at me with sweat gliding over his temples. How long was I out?

"I thought I went too far that time," he whispers as he leans over me again. His pelvis curves and his thrusts slow. "Can you come before you black out again?"

"Yes," I whisper. I don't know if it's the truth, but I'm happy to keep trying.

He leans back and grips my hips, pulling me against him as he fucks me senseless. I think he's giving me time to build up and crest the waves of pleasure, but then his hand wraps around my throat again. He plays with the sides of my neck, the blood chokes giving me a dizzying wave of pleasure that's different from the breath chokes.

He places the collar over my clit again and I moan, my hips bucking against him because I want more. My fingers scramble to press the button, but I mash the wrong one. A sharp vibration buzzes against my clit. I alternate between zapping myself stupid and those pleasurable vibrations as he increases the tempo of his thrusts.

"I'm close," I pant. "I'm so close. Please don't stop."

I'm plunged into dizzying darkness once more as he squeezes my throat. I focus on the pleasure instead of the silence in my lungs. They start to squeeze, warning me of an impending blackout.

"Come, whore, because I won't let go if you don't. You'll die around my cock."

His buttery-soft words don't hold a threat. They hold a fucked-up promise.

I press the button repeatedly, and I fly. My eyes roll back in my head, my legs quiver, and I lose all control of my hands. The remote slides off the bed, but I don't care. I don't need it anymore. His cock is enough to keep me here, riding this wave of pleasure.

A feral growl precedes his gravelly voice. "Oh, there you go. Good fucking girl."

He loosens his grip as my orgasm wanes, but then his fingers tighten and he keeps his hold on my neck until I pass out again. When I come to, he's leaning over me, his belly pressed against mine. Wetness slides between my legs, and I can only assume it's a mixture of our pleasure.

His hand leaves my throat and hooks around the back of my neck with a softness I don't expect. He leans closer. "I know I said I don't kiss whores, but you're too fucking good."

His lips capture mine in a kiss that takes my breath away again. His tongue explores my mouth, and I whimper from the veracity in his motions. Kane might hate me, but Tobin doesn't.

I bathe in his affection as he wipes the tears from my face—my body's innate response to having the life choked from me. He pushes his tear-coated fingers into his mouth and sucks before making me taste it too. Then he pulls out of me, climbs down my body, and stops between my legs. He catches all the mess on his tongue.

His come.

Mine.

And because he clearly can't end on a nice note—which is fine with me—he fists my hair and pulls me up to meet his mouth. He gestures to my lips with his chin, and my lips part as I accept the remnants of our pleasure onto my tongue. I hold my tongue out and waggle it before swallowing.

"You're such a dirty fucking girl," he says. "I love it."

When a dude fucks you like Tobin does, it's too easy to

fall in love with him. It's just hard when that person is inside a person you fucking despise.

As he puts on his pants and slides the leggings over my skin, I have to accept the truth. All doubt is gone. They are three separate men in one body. And one of those men wants me dead.

Chapter Sixteen

Kane

Each rattle of the handcuffs grates against my raw nerves, but I don't trust her to stay put. I even moved her to the front seat so I could keep an eye on her. She has more grit than the girls I usually pick up, and she's a fair bit more intelligent as well. I wouldn't put it past her to figure out how to escape the cuffs if left alone for too long, so I've tethered her to the passenger door. You can't see the glint of metal unless you're looking over her lap.

Pup sits obediently between us, and I reach down and stroke her head. When I was little, I always wanted a dog. Something menacing, like a Doberman. My father never let me have one, and it's comical that I ended up with this little dog. Not the manliest breed, but she's mean as shit. Kinda like me. Why she seems to like the dropout is beyond me, though.

"Do you plan to tell me where we're going?" she asks. "You said south, but where?"

"Texas."

"That's nowhere near New York," she mutters.

"I see you passed geography. Would you like a fucking cookie?"

Thankfully, that shuts her up.

More specifically, we're heading toward Houston, but she doesn't need to know the details. Especially the part where we meet The Nameless.

I didn't keep in touch with the brothers after high school. I happened upon one of them by chance in the produce aisle at a store in our hometown. Even sketchy middlemen need to shop for groceries, I guess. As we were catching up, I disclosed my current profession, and he asked me to move some merchandise for them. I soon found out the merchandise was, in fact, women.

It rubbed me the wrong way at first, but then I found the right motivation. The truck of my dreams. I didn't have enough credit on my own, but The Nameless have connections. And now I owe them.

I think they're Russian, but I've never asked, just like I've never asked the name of their operation. It's better if I don't know. They direct the women to their next destination, often out of this country, and I get a little shaved off my debt.

I can't wait to hand this one off. The few acceptable specimens I've brought to The Nameless sat shivering in fear in the corner, too afraid to take a step out of place. I didn't even have to cuff them. This one? She has too much . . . something. Something that makes her very difficult to break. I want to call it bravery, but it could be stupidity for all I know. Either way, I have to be way too careful around her, and I don't like it.

I'm also sick of tending to her. She has to piss every few

miles, and she's always hungry. If she keeps this shit up, I'll hand her a bucket and a pack of crackers and tell her to make it work. There isn't a word to describe how much I can't stand her.

Tobin fucking *loves* her, though. He left a note basically saying as much. *I choked her nearly to death and she came from it.* That's his love language. Choking and fucking.

Jax started simping over her the moment we saw her, so there's no question that he's attached. And that's a fucking problem. His purpose is to protect me, so what happens when we have a conflict of interest?

She's causing dysfunction in my system, and I don't appreciate it.

In the end, both of my alters will have to let go of something they've grown close to. We can't keep her. Even if I could get past my distaste for her, I've already promised her to someone else. Someone who could cause a lot of problems for me if I back out. Jax and Tobin will have to get over it. We have Pup. We don't need another pet.

I've been keeping a close eye on my phone. When they've lined up the buyer, they'll let me know. Then it's only a matter of completing the drive and handing her off. I'll celebrate afterward. I might even pick up another girl. Jax can talk sweet to her, Tobin can fuck her, and then I can kill her. All will be right with the world.

"I've never been to Kentucky before," she says as she looks out the window. "We should try the fried chicken while we're here."

"This isn't a fucking vacation."

"I'm well aware." She wiggles her wrist, and the metal-on-metal sound rakes a nail across my brain. "Still, we have to eat at some point. Don't you ever get hungry?"

I do, but not for anything I can pick up at a roadside establishment.

A sign lights up as we approach. It signals me to turn off at an inspection site a few miles ahead. Fuck. I can't handle people. If they only asked one question, I could manage, but sometimes they hold us up for an hour or more while they nitpick everything about the truck and our logs. When my patience runs thin, I'm not the best at masking it. That's Jax's specialty.

I feel the tap behind my eyes, and I know I need to relinquish control to him. There's only one fucking problem. The last time I let him have control, he let the girl run off. What if she rats us out? How will Jax handle that? Because she absolutely will rat me out.

But maybe not Jax.

The wheels in my brain begin to turn as an idea forms. Sweet son of a bitch that he is, she might have a little sympathy for him. And it might be just enough to keep her pouty lips sealed. I'm taking a risk either way. If I let him have control, he might set her free, but if I don't, she might try to set herself free by blowing the whistle.

Sweat coats my hands as my grip tightens around the steering wheel. I try to control my breathing, but my chest feels like someone is wringing my lungs in their hands. I can't skip the stop. I'm guaranteed a shitstorm if I pass by.

I have no choice but to let him out. No choice but to let him protect us all.

Chapter Seventeen

Aurora

I can't take my eyes off him as he rubs his hands on his jeans, wearing the denim to a lighter shade with each pass. Sweat gathers at his temples. I don't know what has him so shaken up, but he's starting to make me a bit antsy as well. When his anxious, hardened expression loosens, I can only assume he's switched.

"Hey, sweet girl," he says, low and soft, and I know exactly who he is now. Jax has taken over.

I haven't seen him since he let me escape. Maybe Kane punished him by keeping him back. A sliver of guilt winds through me, snaking past my heart and settling low in my stomach. It coils there, tightening and writhing until it's a physical thing I can't ignore. Even though it's technically Kane's fault for picking me up and holding me hostage, I'm causing problems for all of them.

I shake my head. Do I actually believe this shit?

I hate to admit I am, but I can't deny the reality in front of my face. Hearing about people with alters is one thing.

Seeing someone with this condition for a few minutes on social media or television isn't the same as living with them for days. The differences between the three men are undeniable and wholly total. He is Kane. He is Jax. He is Tobin.

But why?

From what very little I've heard about this condition, its cause is often rooted in trauma. We brushed over it in psychology, and I wrack my mind now for what I learned, but I only come up with questions instead of answers. What sort of hammer smashed his psyche to the point of fracture? Who hurt him?

Kane won't answer these questions, so I make a mental note to try to get information from the other two.

"Jax?" I ask, just to be sure.

"The one and only," he says with a smile.

We pass a blinking sign that signals an inspection station ahead. Is that what had Kane so on edge? If so, Jax doesn't share the same phobia. Once he wipes his forehead, it stays dry, and his hands relax on the steering wheel.

When he finally glances over at me, he sucks in a sharp breath. "Oh shit, is that from . . ." He shakes his head. "I never should have let you run off."

My hand goes to my throat. He must have noticed the marks. "I had to try, Jax. You understand that, right?"

He pulls over on the shoulder and unclips his seatbelt. After rifling through the cabinets in the back, he returns with a lacy scarf. Whose? I probably don't want to know.

Jax leans over. His fingers trace the marks from the choke collar before covering the bruises with the lace. He knots it on the side, and he doesn't need to tell me why. He doesn't want anyone to see the marks and get suspicious.

This creates a problem in my mind. We'll stop at the inspection site, and someone will give the truck a once over.

I've been through this before with other truckers, and I won't pretend it doesn't present an opportunity to escape this hell once and for all. But will I take that opportunity?

For Kane's part in this mess, I'm inclined to scream bloody murder the moment the inspector approaches the truck. I can end it all right now. But Kane isn't the only person this would affect. Jax and Tobin are part and parcel, and I'm conflicted. Jax has let me go, and Tobin's only guilty of giving me incredible orgasms. Is it fair to condemn them for the acts of their splintered mind?

And what if I don't rat them out? Perhaps I can play the long game and win Kane's trust.

To scream or not to scream. That is the question.

Jax leans into me. "Do me a favor, sweet girl. Don't blow our cover at this inspection. I . . . did very unwell in prison."

He's laying the guilt on thick, and I'm not immune. I don't believe he deserves to waste away in a cell, and neither does Tobin. But I want to live. Kane hasn't killed me yet, but that's the keyword.

Yet.

Jax places his fingers on my chin and draws me into him. As he kisses me, I'm reminded of the differences between him and Tobin. He's gentle and sweet, giving more than he takes from me. Instead of tongue-fucking my mouth like Tobin, his kiss comforts me. I melt into it against my will. My lip quivers as he pulls away from me. He isn't making this decision any easier.

He grabs the blanket and puts it across my lap, covering my handcuffed wrist before dropping back to his seat and eyeing me with an approving nod. As he buttons his flannel, he looks like a teenager trying to hide his tattoos from his parents. He looks in the mirror and smooths his hair. Satisfied that he appears as respectable as possible, he rolls back onto the road and heads toward the inspection site.

Two DOT vans crouch at the head of the pull off, and I imagine flagging down the people inside. My brain can't fathom what would happen if I acted on this impulse. Would Kane give up, or would a chase ensue?

Jax pulls to a stop, and a DOT officer appears in the window.

"License?" the officer asks.

Jax pulls out his CDL license and hands it over.

"Thanks, Mr. Hargrave," the officer says before leaning closer to Jax, probably trying to smell if he's been drinking. "Triangles and fire extinguisher?"

"Excuse me," Jax says, and the man outside the window hops from the side of the truck, giving him room to open the door.

Jax climbs out and pulls the fire extinguisher from beneath his seat. The officer checks it over to make sure it's charged before putting it back in its rightful place. The safety triangles are kept in a side box behind the door, and Jax has to step away from the truck to access them. The DOT officer remains just outside the door, and I can't tear my eyes away from him. Everything in me screams that this is my chance to signal for help.

If I'm going to do it, I'm running out of time.

Satisfied with the gear, the officer glances at me. "Along for the ride?"

Now's my chance. The words climb up my throat.

I've been kidnapped. He wants to kill me. Well, not this guy, but the other guy that shares the same body and brain. Maybe I'll leave that part out. All I have to do is kick this blanket away and rip off the scarf with my free hand.

But I nod. "Yep, just keeping him company."

The officer's eyes narrow. "You okay, miss?"

"Oh, yeah, I'm fine. Just pretty tired. We've been on the road for a bit."

The officer nods and turns back to Jax. "Can I see your bills and logs?"

Jax leans over and grabs a stack of papers and hands it to him. "Should all be there. We're dead-heading right now. On our way to pick up a load in Texas."

As he settles in his seat, a light sweat pricks my brow.

Jax buckles his seatbelt as the DOT officer disappears around the side of the truck. "You're doing so good," he says.

He wouldn't say that if he knew what was running through my mind. I still have a chance to get away, and I'm not completely sure I won't take it.

Pup jumps into my lap and settles against the blanket. A low growl rumbles in her tiny chest each time the officer speaks. A glint of silver catches my eye, and I realize she's moved the blanket and exposed the handcuff. I could leave it. If the officer sees it, that wouldn't be entirely my fault.

With my free hand, I pull the blanket over my wrist once more.

The man returns to the window and hands the paperwork and the DOT inspection report to Jax. "You're good to go."

"Thank you, officer. Have a great day!" Jax says, and I truly can't imagine Kane saying such a thing.

As the truck begins to pull away, the vans and the people grow smaller in the mirror. For a moment, it's still not too late. I could lower the window and scream. I could save myself. But I don't, and the figures shrink until they're only memories as we pull onto the road once more.

I shift in my seat, and Pup sighs as she settles in for a nap. I stroke her fur and fight back tears. An opportunity just slipped through my fingers, and I don't know that another will grace my path. I don't even know how long my path is. Everything could end in ten miles, or it could continue for eternity. I have to find a way to survive that doesn't involve hurting Jax or Tobin, and maybe that starts with discovering why Kane is the way he is.

"What is Kane hiding?" I say.

"Best not to ask."

I lick my lips and play my cards. "I just did you a huge favor. Instead of blowing the whistle, I kept my mouth shut. Can't you reciprocate a little?"

He shifts in his seat and shakes his head. "It doesn't work like that."

"Then how does it work?" I blow out a breath and look out the window. "If you can't answer the big question, at least explain why you had to handle the inspection. Give me some insight."

He considers this, then deems it safe to answer. "Kane doesn't do well with people. I'm a people person."

Pup hops down and trots to the back of the truck as I stare at him. I throw the blanket off my lap. I'm burning up, mostly from sheer frustration. "Why do you protect him?"

His lips tighten. "That's what I was made for."

"What does that even mean?"

He chews the inside of his lip. "When the main system goes through something so traumatic that they can't mentally handle it, they need someone else to. That's where I came from. I was born to protect Kane."

"Really?" I ask. I'm not trying to sound that way, but it just all seems so far-fetched to me. Like something out of a movie. Except this is real life.

My life.

"You don't have to believe me," Jax says. "A lot of people

don't. Not that we tell very many people about us. I think you're the first girl."

My chest rises in defiance. "Because no one else lives long enough to find out?"

Jax smirks. "There's no point telling anyone who wouldn't understand."

"And what makes you so sure I can?"

He shrugs his shoulders. "Trauma recognizes trauma. You aren't fragmented the same way we are, but you're just as broken."

I think back to my childhood. To the dorms at college. And I realize . . . he's right.

Chapter Eighteen

Kane

We drive by the sign for my favorite diner between here and my hometown in Texas. I've taken these interstate systems a million times, and I'll take them a million times more. By now, these highways are as familiar as the veins in my arm. I could drive this route in my sleep.

My eyes harden on the sign. The corners have begun to peel away from the metal, but that doesn't dictate the state of the food, which is always fucking incredible. Mashed potatoes that are just stiff enough to stick to your ribs but soft enough to go down smooth. Steaks seasoned to mouth-watering perfection. And the steamed broccoli. I don't normally enjoy green vegetables—I'm a meat and potatoes kind of guy—but the cheese sauce they slather over the little green stalks is like liquid pleasure. Aside from killing, eating at the diner is the closest I'll ever come to having an orgasm.

I'm fucking starving. That much is clear. I can't remember the last time I sat down and had a good meal without being disturbed, but it's been too long. My head is quiet for once, so I take the turn and head toward the diner.

Dropout rattles the handcuff on her wrist. She stares straight ahead as if she'd like to be anywhere else, which is probably accurate, but she needs to learn her place. She's with me now, and that won't change until I hand her off in Texas.

Meeting The Nameless isn't my only reason for heading back to Texas, and Jax wasn't lying when I spoke to the DOT officer. I managed to broker a load between here and Texas, which means I need to clean out the trailer before we get there. Having a reefer unit means the distributors want proof of a clean trailer before they stock perishables inside. Which means I need to actually *clean* that trailer before I get there. It's dirty in more ways than one.

"You're bringing me back to New York after this, right?" she asks.

"Sure," I say. It's a lie to keep the bitch calm for my sanity. And hers, I guess. Is it wrong to feed her little nibbles of hope for the rest of the trip? I can only see the benefits. It will—hopefully—stop her from running off again, which means I can sleep without keeping one eye open. If she needs to think this is a detour on our way to New York, then so be it.

I pull into the truck stop and stare at the sign for the diner. I can already smell the sizzling meat

"You gonna be good, dropout?"

"Stop calling me that."

I grip her chin. "Are you gonna be good?"

When she doesn't respond, I tighten my grip and nod her head for her. If she isn't good, she should already know what will happen to her. Yeah, I've already sold her to The

Nameless, but I have no problem doing what I love if she can't act right. She'd look even prettier dead.

I unchain her wrist, and she rubs the sensitive ring of red skin. I may need to keep her untethered when we're on the road. If she gets an infection or gets too dinged up, The Nameless won't give me enough for her.

We get out of the truck, and I grab her arm to keep her close to my side. "Look like you want to be here," I say, jabbing my fingers into her side.

"I absolutely want to be here, thank you very much. I'm sick of munching on the expired gas station food you've stashed in the cabinets like some sort of psychotic squirrel."

I almost smile at her little jab. She's got spunk, I'll give her that.

We walk inside, and a bell tolls overhead. A familiar waitress scurries around behind the counter. She's nearly always at her station when I visit, almost as if she lives here. Her graying black hair sits in stressed curls on her head, and she glances up as we pass the counter.

"Kane, how long has it been?" she asks, a hint of flirt in her eyes. This poor old hound is baying up the wrong tree. If I have no attraction to Aurora, she doesn't have a chance in hell. I've never been attracted to anyone. Not like that, at least.

"A year? Maybe more," I say as I sit in the booth farthest from the door. Aurora sits across from me. Her hands go into her lap, and she stares out the large window beside our booth.

"Your daughter?" the waitress asks, her eyes falling on Aurora. I kick her beneath the table, and she turns toward the woman with a fake smile.

"Yes, ma'am," Aurora answers, her whore-customer-service voice coming out to play. It's repulsive.

The waitress drops the menus in front of me, and I hand one to Aurora.

"Thanks . . . Daddy," she says with a snarky smile.

I didn't think I looked old enough to be her father, but I guess that's a better answer than trying to explain she's a whore I picked up to potentially sell. Or kill.

The waitress takes her notepad from her raggedy apron and wrestles out the pen that's speared itself through the newest hole. "Mashed potatoes, steamed broccoli with cheese, and a steak, very rare," she spouts before I can open my mouth.

"That's exactly right," I say. I like my meat like I like my women—bloody and raw. When the waitress turns toward Aurora, I speak for her. "Same for her. But make it medium-well."

She seems like a medium-well kind of girl.

The waitress nods and heads toward the back. Aurora and I sit in painful silence while waiting for our meal. I don't usually have to force a conversation with these bitches. Mostly, they just beg for their lives and I mock their final breaths.

"Who's the 'daddy'?" she asks, pointing to the tattoo on my neck.

"What?"

"Who got the daddy tattoo? The one on your neck. Was it Tobin or you? It certainly wasn't Jax."

I don't answer her. I just tap the fork on the cracked tabletop. Her face draws into a tight frown; the sound clearly drives her nuts. I can't kill her, but I sure enjoy irritating her. And degrading her. I just wish she reacted more to the degradation. If she wasn't such a stoic whore, she'd almost be tolerable. Since I'm finally getting a rise out of her, I tap the metal harder.

She slams her eyes shut. "Can you stop?"

I point the fork at her. "You suck off the handle of a urinal without a peep of protest, but this is what bothers you?"

She glances around the diner as a few people stare at her because of what I've just said . . . a little too loudly. Heat flushes her cheeks, and I revel in her embarrassment. It's not as good as choking the life out of her, but it's enjoyable.

"Why are you the way you are?" she clips in a whisper. "Have you ever thought about trying to be even a little pleasant to be around?"

A lot has happened to me to make me the way I am, but I can't answer her question. It's something I've asked myself many times, but that locked box just remains locked. I am walking, talking evil, but the source of that black fountain is buried too deep.

"I'm incapable of pleasantry," I say.

"Bullshit. I've seen exactly what you're capable of."

I laugh, knowing exactly what she's referring to. "Jax and I are *not* the same person. We may share a body, but we couldn't be more different. He's a disgusting little simp, and I'm not."

I couldn't be like Jax, mentally or physically. Despite him holding pieces of my trauma, he's so kind. And he can fuck. He probably likes pleasing a woman and making love. Jax is the light I could never shine on this world.

He and Tobin are capable of emotions I have no desire to feel. Integration is possible for many people with dissociative identity disorder, but it has never been my end goal. Our system works for us, even if it's a little fucked-up to everyone else. But that's the beauty of it. It isn't meant for everyone else. It's a safety plan designed just for us. We compartmentalize in ways most others can't, and that's how we continue to function.

Or it was how we functioned until Aurora came along. Her attitude is like a screwdriver for me. Her pussy is like a drill for Tobin. Her beauty and charisma are a hammer and nails for Jax. Without even trying, she's tinkering with our machine. If we aren't careful, if Jax and Tobin can't get on the same page with me, we're fucked.

Chapter Nineteen

Aurora

Spit gathers beneath my tongue as Kane's eyes darken. I swallow it down. I tried to get him to loosen the fuck up, but having a nice conversation or sharing banter doesn't seem to be in his wheelhouse. Bringing up his alters like that was probably a low blow, but it's not my fault they're more enjoyable than he could ever be. They're the only reason I'm still alive. They're also the only reason I'm not screaming for help right now.

The waitress appears beside our table and sets our plates in front of us. I start to eat, looking away from Kane as he dives into his bloody steak like he hasn't eaten in a month. When he finally slows down, red-tinged grease drips from his lower lip. He stares at me as he sensually licks it away. It's not meant to be a sensual gesture, though. It's meant to be intimidating. It's meant to scare me.

That's just too bad. I don't scare easily.

I reach across, stab my knife and fork into his steak, and cut a piece away. I rip it off the fork, open my mouth, stick out my tongue, and squeeze the hunk of meat until red juice drips into my mouth. A metallic tang hits my tastebuds.

My little act seems to work. He goes back to gnawing on his slab of E. coli, and I return to pushing my fork through the pile of mashed potatoes.

I've always been stubborn, but I've never been quite as bullheaded as I am when I'm going against Kane. He brings it out of me. The more he tries to break me down, the more I refuse to let him. Even if he breaks me on the inside, I'll never show it to him. I'll die with a smile on my face before I give him a glimpse of my discomfort. He'll have to do worse than what he's tried so far if he wants to break someone who's already used to bending.

My stomach churns with each bite I take, but I clean my plate. There's no telling when I'll be treated to another meal like this. We're almost in Tennessee now, and I don't know if he'll drive straight on to Texas from here. Part of me hopes so. The sooner we get to Texas, the closer I am to making my way back to New York.

Thoughts of my parents burrow into my chest and squeeze my heart. These aren't fond thoughts. Fear shrouds my brain. Telling them what I've done—leaving college and becoming a sex worker—isn't possible, but I don't know how to explain what I've been through. Even if I figure out what to say, they won't hear it. And if my father has been drinking—

"I'm going to go pay," he says, his eyes narrowing on me. "Cut what's left of my steak into small pieces and wrap it in a napkin."

I clear my throat and nod as he eases out of the booth. Once I've done as he asked and packed the leftover meat into the napkin, I turn to look at him. He stands at the register, locked in a conversation with the waitress. I could make a run for it, but I probably wouldn't make it across the diner before he stopped me, and something tells me the waitress wouldn't believe anything that would cast her little crush in a bad light.

If I wanted to escape, I should have said something at the inspection site. So what does that say about me? Do I really plan to stick with these guys until my fate is revealed? Because I'm still not sure what happens at the end of the line. He could kill me. He could drive me to New York.

Neither option appeals to me.

With a deep sigh, I slide out of the booth. "Let's go . . . Daddy," I say as I come up behind him.

He fakes a smile, takes the napkin, and stuffs it into his pocket, then wraps an arm around me. His muscles tense as our bodies make contact, which tells me he's not used to close human interaction.

"Come on, sweetie," he says, and it's the most uncomfortable thing I've ever heard leave a man's lips. He isn't meant to say nice fucking things. That much is clear.

He keeps up the act as we walk outside, but his lips tighten and he releases me a few steps onto the asphalt. As he lifts his shoe, a trail of gum tethers him to the concrete.

"Son of a bitch." His gait changes as he guides me to the truck by my hair. Once we're inside, he throws me onto the floor, sits in the driver's seat, and kicks his feet out in front of him. "Clean my boots," he commands.

Jesus fucking Christ. This guy.

I don't move at first. I just stare up at him. He can't be serious.

"Crawl to me and lick my boots clean. If I have to say it again, I'll shove my boot down your goddamn throat."

I crawl over to him. *Just do it,* I pep-talk myself.

He picks up the boot that doesn't have the gum on it

and steps on my neck, pushing me to the ground as he grinds the leather sole into my throat. He puts the other boot by my mouth, and I force out my tongue to lick the side of his shoe. The rich scents of leather and polish rush toward my nose. It tastes how it smells, like a natural musk.

His boot hovers over my face as he pulls it back a few inches and releases the other boot from my neck. A glob of blue gum sticks to the bottom. I try not to think about the mouth who chewed this gum. I try not to think about the pavement it was stuck to and all the feet that walked across it. I just arch my neck, lift my mouth to the gum, and rip it from the rubber. It spreads into thin strings, but it eventually lets go and lands on my tongue. A very subtle mint flavor lingers in the glob, and an earthy note from the ground follows it.

I refuse to gag. I won't give him the satisfaction.

"Chew it and swallow it," he says as he leans back.

"You don't want me to blow a bubble too?"

I roll my eyes and do as I'm told. He reaches down, and I cock my head at him before he shakes his wrist, encouraging me to take his hand. Stunned, I allow him to help me to my feet.

He leans closer, and his breath rushes over my ear. "I got the tattoo. I like when you bitches call me daddy."

For some reason, I don't believe him. Maybe he doesn't want to admit that someone like Tobin has more control over what's on his body than he does.

Kane whistles for Pup, and she leaps off the bed, trots to his side, and sits obediently at his feet. Her tail thumps against the floor as he pulls the napkin from his pocket and feeds her his leftovers.

"Good girl," he whispers, trying to keep me from hearing his momentary softness. But I definitely heard it, and I can't pretend I'm not running those gentle words through my mind now.

Good girl.

Kane kicks off his now-clean boots and drags me toward the bed. He pushes me onto the mattress, and I think Tobin has taken over. He still looks like Kane, though. The mannerisms, the way he moves. Then he speaks, and I'm sure he's still Kane.

"Time for bed, dropout," he says as he unbuttons his shirt. I'd be worried he was going to force himself on me if he didn't look so repulsed by our close proximity.

"We're sleeping in bed together?" I ask, surprised.

"I can't sleep in the seat anymore. My back is killing me. So yeah, I guess so."

I get into bed and lie as close to the wall as I can. He crawls in behind me and sighs as he turns away from me. His posture is so rigid and uncomfortable, and at this moment, I'm not sure who the captive is. Me or him.

Chapter Twenty

Tobin

Kane's so dramatic. He couldn't even handle lying beside the girl for five fucking minutes. Instead of sleeping on a mattress, Kane felt as if he were lying on a bed of nails. The moment I heard his thoughts, I was ready to climb into the driver's seat. She may disgust him, but I'm obsessed with everything about her.

Now that I'm here, I don't see what the big deal was. She's turned away from me on her side, and with all this distance between us, I wouldn't even consider this as sleeping in the same bed. I move closer until my chest presses against her back and her ass bumps against my crotch.

"Hi, Tobin," she mumbles, her voice heavy with sleep.

"How'd you know it was me?"

"Because Kane would rather die than touch me, and Jax has too much couth to put his hard dick against my ass."

"Fair," I say with a dark laugh. Jax would be sweeter about it. He'd talk to her, wipe the hair from her pretty cheeks, and ask fucking permission before touching her. But I'm not a wait-for-permission kind of guy when it comes to her. She's a need, not a want.

"I'm glad you're here, though," she says, and my heart pumps harder—no one has ever said they were glad to see me—but my feeling of elation dissipates when she speaks again. "I wanted to talk to you about something. About Kane."

"I'm not really the talking type. I'm the fuck-you-senseless type, remember?"

I put my arm around her, raise my hand to her mouth, and shove my fingers past her lips. Before she even knows what's happening, my fingertips reach the back of her throat and a violent gag rattles her body. Instead of reaching for my wrists and pulling me away, she rolls onto her back and swirls her tongue across my skin.

This is what I mean when I say I'm obsessed. She's like no other woman I've met. This girl will take anything I give her.

I lean over her and finger-fuck her mouth, and she bites down as her big eyes rise to mine. Pain heats my knuckles, but I don't pull them away. She and I both know how much I enjoy pain.

"You have such a good mouth, eighty," I say as I pull my fingers away. "I'd just prefer you use it for something other than talking right now."

She takes the hint and doesn't ask anything else as I get up to go to the freezer. I pull out two of my special ice cubes and put them in a glass.

Sitting up on her elbows, she eyes the milky cubes. "What are you doing with those?"

"You'll find out soon enough," I say with a smirk.

I kneel beside her on the bed and grab the hem of her

dress shirt. Like the obedient little slut she is, she raises her arms and allows me to pull it away. I pull away the leggings next, and now only her panties separate me from what I want most.

She whimpers as I grip the thin fabric and rip it away from her body. I grab one of the ice cubes and I trace the outline of her lips, coating them with a glistening layer of come and water. As I drag the ice lower and run it over her breasts, her nipples pull into tight buds. They practically beg for my mouth, so I oblige.

Her legs pull together as my hand trails toward the curve of her lower abdomen. The skin and muscle suck inward, trying to escape the icy chill, but I keep going. Lower. Lower. I release her breast from my mouth and slide down her body so I can put myself between her legs. Her pretty little clit swells for me as the ice cube drifts over it.

She whimpers as I part her legs wider and push her knees toward the mattress, tilting her hips upward. Come-laced water cuts a path through her slit and drips over her tight little asshole. It's the only thing I haven't taken.

I lean back and gather spit beneath my tongue before dripping the saliva onto her hole. I push the ice cube into her pussy, knowing her heat will soon reduce it to a puddle that will slowly seep out of her. She screams out from the cold, and in the same breath, I put a finger in her ass. Then two. A groan leaves my lips as I push a third inside her.

Her body fights the intrusion before relaxing and accepting the pleasure my touch provides. When I'm sure she's ready, I remove my pants, coat my dick tattoo with saliva, and push inside her. My barbell catches on the rim of her ass, and her back arches as pain rips through her, but I fight past her body's noes until they become a unified yes. A well-trained whore like her knows how to take what is given, and it's not like I would stop anyway.

I want her full of me, so I reach over and grab the remaining ice cube, leaving behind a thin layer of cloudy liquid at the bottom of the glass. While continuing to thrust inside her ass, I run the melting cube over her lips again.

"Say my name before I fill your mouth."

"Tobin." She pants through the pain and pleasure rushing through her in equal measure.

"Now open," I command.

She spreads her lips and I drop the ice cube onto her tongue. Her eyes close and her expression twists for a moment before she gathers her composure and sucks on the cube. Her cheeks pull inward as she swirls the ice around in her mouth. She's such a stoic whore, and it's so fucking sexy.

I shove two fingers inside her pussy as I fuck her ass. With each moan that slips past her parted lips, a little of the come-water mixture slips from the side of her mouth and dribbles down her chin. What a good fucking cum-slut.

My thumb grazes her clit as I finger her. I have to stop thrusting because knowing she's so filled with me brings me too close. It's a majestic fucking sight. She curls her abdomen as her orgasm builds, and she tightens around my fingers and cock.

"Are you going to come for me, eighty? With your mouth and cunt filled with my come?"

She nods, her lips puckering as she sucks on the ice cube.

"Good girl," I growl as she shudders around me.

Her muscles clench around my dick, and I can't wait any longer. I lean onto my outstretched arm and fuck her until I spill my load inside her. I stay inside her ass as I pull her mouth to mine and kiss her, regardless of the residue in her mouth. I can't help the desire to mark her.

My hand leaves her cunt and winds through her hair as I pull her into me. When her lips spread, she tongues the mixture into my mouth. The taste is salty and foul, but I happily take what she gives me.

I pull out of her and look down. My gaze oscillates between her wet lips and the dripping mess leaking from her pussy and the thin white ropes gracing her tight asshole. She's fucking stunning.

I drop to my knees, lift her hips, and bring her ass closer to my mouth. Leaning over her creamy, come-filled hole, I let my tongue slip into her ass. She's stretched and used up, and I love it. Eating pussy is a Jax move, but I'll eat her come-filled asshole all day.

A feral groan leaves her lips from having my tongue on such a sensitive part of her body. A part of us all that's so neglected. It creates such a taboo thrill to know you aren't supposed to be buried between someone's ass cheeks, but here you are, doing it and loving it.

I lick her clean of my come. Her come. The melted ice.

"You like when I lick your ass, eighty?"

"Yes," she pants.

She turns over on her hands and knees and backs her ass into me. This dirty fucking girl knows what she wants. I grip her ass cheeks, spread them, and eat her as her fingers work her clit.

"Lick me, Tobin," she moans. She swirls her fingers, and my tongue works her until she comes again.

I pull away from her and look down at perfection. Fuck Kane. He doesn't know what he's missing with her. Fucking her is like sinking into a fallen angel. If he actually fucked her, there'd be no way he could get rid of her. If I had any say, I would never let her go. She'd be my come-filled fuck toy.

She'd be mine.

Aurora rolls onto her back, her chest heaving up and down as she tries to catch her breath. "Now can we talk?"

The sex only derailed her thoughts momentarily. She's already back on track, barreling toward the station at full speed, and I don't know how much longer I can dance around the topic. I sit beside her on the bed, unable to look at her as I speak.

"He's been through some shit. He doesn't know exactly what, because I keep those painful memories locked away from him. I can't risk telling you because I can't risk *you* telling *him*."

I expect a huff of indifference or an argument, but she only places a hand against my back and rubs in comforting circles. "Kane's lucky to have you and Jax," she says. "I wish I had someone to hold my trauma."

"What have you been through?" I ask.

Her hand stops moving. "Some shit," she says, throwing my words back at me.

Fair enough. It wouldn't be right to expect her to spill her secrets when I keep ours locked away.

I rise from the bed and begin to dress. "If you ever change your mind, let me know. I'm pretty good at holding trauma."

"Thanks, Tobin," she whispers.

Looking back at her, I can't imagine letting her go. Kane still has a chance to stop the boulder he's started rolling down a hill, so I walk to the stack of sticky notes and think of what to write that might change his mind. We make plenty of money and we'll have this truck paid off in a couple of years. Selling her would shave off a few months at most. Even if we can't keep her, I'd rather know she's somewhere safe and not beneath the sort of men The Nameless rub elbows with.

Because I'll always see her as mine.

Ours.

But what would possibly convince Kane to see her as Jax and I do? His hatred for women stems from a secret he can't remember, and I can't reveal that secret without risking his mind. If he knew the truth of his hatred, he might understand that Aurora is not a threat to him. If anything, she could be his salvation.

Then my phone vibrates in my pocket and changes everything. It's a text from The Nameless. They've found a buyer.

Chapter Twenty-One

Kane

I wake up beside her, with Pup curled between us. The dropout smells clean, which means Tobin probably took her inside the truck stop and let her shower. That was a terrible idea. I don't trust that he can keep her from running off. Then again, maybe she was too thoroughly fucked to run.

I lift the collar of my shirt and inhale. I smell clean too. What sort of shit did we get into last night that would cause both of us to need a shower? Neither of them better bond too closely with each other, because this little arrangement isn't permanent. Frankly, I can't wait to get rid of her.

A dull ache pulses through the muscles in my back and ass as I climb out of bed. I'm getting too old for Tobin to fuck like we're still in our twenties. That ship has sailed.

I grab a glass and set it on the counter with a loud clink. I refuse to tiptoe around and keep quiet so she can continue drifting through dreamland. Rise and shine, dropout.

I open the fridge and pull out the milk. I pour some into

the glass and take a sip. It's not warm, but it's not cold enough for me.

Aurora stirs, turning over and staring at me. Her eyes drop to the glass.

"That's your breakfast?" she asks, stretching.

I nod. I've had a glass of milk every morning for as long as I can remember. I used to wake up before my parents and pour a glass before they got up. It was my moment of calm before heading into a shitstorm each day. I stare at her as I pull out the ice tray and absentmindedly grab the few remaining cubes.

"Um . . ." she says, and I narrow my eyes on her.

"What the fuck's your problem?"

She smirks. "Actually, nothing."

I drop the ice cubes into the milk, swirl the glass, and take a sip. A pungent flavor hits my tongue. Like old beer and something else. I barely make it to the sink before I spit it out.

"Honestly, I struggled to believe this whole multiple personality thing, but this just solidifies it," she says. "No one would willingly consume those."

I study the glass. "What was in the ice cubes?"

"Tobin's jizz," she says with a laugh.

I know it's Tobin's because it sure as shit isn't mine, and Jax wouldn't dream of coming in the ice tray. Despite how annoyed I am, my lips threaten to pull into a smile. It's her infectious laugh.

"I'm glad you find this so funny," I say as I pour out the milk.

"It's kinda hilarious."

Turning away from her, I allow my lips to pull into a smile. It's a foreign feeling, but I can't pretend I don't like the way it feels. People smile every day. People smile all the time. But not me. I haven't had anything to smile about in a very long time. Maybe ever.

I pull out my phone to check the time, and I notice a text from The Nameless. They found a buyer for the girl, which means there's no backing out now. In a few short days, she'll be off my hands and I'll be free to do as I please again.

So why don't I feel good about it?

I blame Tobin and Jax. Though our system is demarcated by deep lines that keep us within our respective places, we sometimes experience emotional bleed-through. They're upset about the finality of this text. They know what it means. Well, fuck them. I'm happy about it, and I remind myself of that as she rises from the bed.

She's wearing one of my t-shirts, and as she bends over to collect her discarded clothes from the floor, I see that the t-shirt is *all* she's wearing. Something far worse than a smile happens within my body as I watch her put on the leggings. There's a tightening in my jeans as I harden for the first time in years.

My lips draw downward. An erection is a sign of weakness for me. It's an innate bodily desire that leaves me feeling sick. Words flash into my mind, though I don't know why.

Don't get hard. If you do, they'll hurt you.

Whatever happened to me all those years ago has been tucked away from my prying mental fingers, but my cock remembers. It became forever limp. A broken body to go with my broken brain.

Until this moment.

Now it has decided that it wants to work, and it strains against my jeans. Aurora turns to say something to me, but her lips clamp shut as her eyes widen. She stares at my erection.

I glare at her neck and allow myself to think the thoughts racing through my mind. Despite my erection, none of these thoughts are sexual. I imagine wrapping my hands around that slender stretch of flesh and squeezing. My fingertips can already feel the way the bones in her throat will collapse beneath the pressure. I can almost see the light leaving her eyes. I can smell the pungent tang of fear as she fights for a breath that won't come.

And still her eyes remain glued to my erection.

"Goddamn it, dropout!" I scream as I rush toward her. My hand winds through her hair, and I use it like a suitcase handle as I drag her across the cab. The truck door creaks open, and I look outside to see if anyone is around. One other truck stands in the lot, but I see no sign of the driver. They're probably still sleeping.

I put my hand around her mouth and pull her into me as I drag her down the steps and toward the back of my trailer. She doesn't fight my hold on her, which both agitates and pleases me. I don't want her to draw any attention, and fighting me would do that, but does she always have to be so unaffected?

My hand closes around the metal handle outside the trailer door, and I whip it open. Cool air rushes toward us. Once we're safely inside, I release her mouth. She turns to me, confusion muddling her eyes.

"Kane, what did I do?"

"You got in my fucking truck."

"Please don't do this," she pleads, and it's the first time genuine fear has shown on her face.

Maybe it's because she knows what will happen if I leave her ass in here. Wearing nothing more than that t-shirt and the thin leggings, she'll freeze to death. But this isn't about that. I have no plans to kill her, especially not now that I know she's destined for greater things. Leaving her back here is a mind game. She'll be so fucking afraid of me that it will alter her brain chemistry. She won't be able to handle being around me after this.

And that's exactly what both of us need.

I flip on the overhead light, exit the truck, and close the door. After securing the latch on the outside, I shake my head. My reaction to seeing her bare legs and ass has left me confused. She has too much power over me, and I can't have that. I have to be in control at all times because I can't trust the other two nitwits. They lose all control whenever she bats her eyelashes at them.

The temptress may have gotten to Tobin and Jax, but I won't allow her to get to me.

Chapter Twenty-Two

Aurora

Freezing air encompasses my body in an icy hug. The leggings give me a little more protection than the thin t-shirt, but not by much. The weird thing about being trapped in the cold is that it almost feels warm sometimes. Maybe it's the incessant shivering. It's violent enough that my muscles begin to ache after only a few minutes.

I try the door. There's a handle on the inside, but he must have a locking mechanism on the outside, because it doesn't budge. I'm not sure why I thought any different. Considering the random stash of women's clothing and Kane's violent tendencies, I'm probably not the first woman he's stuffed back here.

My feet nearly come out from under me when the truck begins to move. Now I'm faced with the reality of my situation. Kane plans to leave me in here until I'm dead, and I don't even know what I did wrong. That's more frustrating than being locked in a freezer on wheels.

I think back to our interaction. He seemed fine until I turned around and noticed he was hard. I thought Tobin had taken over, but then he got really upset and stuffed me back here. And he called me dropout, which means he was definitely still Kane. So how did he have an erection?

The truck turns, sending me to my ass. It also jostles something near the back of the unit. I turn to get a better look at the mound in the back corner. A faded blue blanket drapes over something lumpy and long. Even though I can't make out what lies beneath the blanket, I know exactly what's peeking from beneath it.

Long, dark hair.

My body leaps backward at the realization, and I slide down the icy side wall as I try to wrap my head around what I've seen. Surely it's just my wild imagination. I'm freezing to death and going insane, but I'm definitely not locked in a small space with a deceased person.

Curiosity gets the best of me, and I crawl toward the mound. I verify my fear as I pull back a crisp blanket and find a dead fucking body.

And she's very dead. Though the cold temperatures have mostly preserved her, a foggy glaze covers her unseeing eyes and her skin has begun to change color. A purplish bruise circles her neck, and I don't need more than one guess to figure out who put it there. I brush the hair away from her face. Wrinkles crease her skin, and smears of dark makeup smudge her cheeks.

I'm alone and there's no one to hide my emotions from this time, so I allow the anger and fear to battle inside me. I'm doing everything I can to stay alive, but will Kane let me live after his nice little trip to Texas? Probably not. I'm doomed to meet the same fate as the poor woman in front of me.

Part of me almost accepts this, but the other part thinks I can win him over. Kane is way more guarded than Jax or Tobin, but I'm willing to do whatever it takes to weasel my way into his mind. Judging by what happened earlier, I'm well on my way to success. I got him hard, though he clearly hated it. But it's a reaction.

Unfortunately, it landed me in this freezer, where I'll probably die from exposure.

Like a terrible human being, I take the blanket off the woman's body and wrap it around myself. It's not like she needs it anymore, but I still feel guilty for taking her shroud. It provides little warmth, but it's better than leaving my arms exposed.

I back into the wall and draw my legs to my chest, curling into a ball. Moments of warmth come over my body, which scare me more than the freezing temperatures. Isn't that what happens when you're in the throes of hypothermia? You feel warm?

Am I going to die here?

It almost seems better to just fall asleep in the cold than to be killed by fucking Kane. It's hard to keep my cool when someone is actively trying to murder me, and I want so desperately to seem like the unbreakable bitch he thinks I am.

In truth, I'm very breakable. A group of frat boys proved that.

In a moment of impending death, I think about what made me run from college. Memories come to me in flashes. Being drunk, hardly able to stand. And then the door to my dorm room opened.

I close my eyes and shut out the memories. Time doesn't heal all wounds.

Shortly after that happened, I left school. I couldn't

focus on class and instead began to drink my feelings away, though I wasn't old enough to get booze. That created its own set of problems, but I found solutions. To numb the ache and the racing thoughts, I needed the alcohol, but to get the alcohol, I had to do favors. That started it all for me. The barter system that comes from having a female body and a need I can't fulfill on my own.

I clearly have very good coping mechanisms.

After my assault, I should have gone home to my parents and gotten sober. I should have allowed myself to heal properly. Maybe get some fucking therapy. Extensively. But I dug myself into a grave of lies, and I didn't have the courage to return.

Maybe going home has been a pipe dream all along. Some stupid goal I set because it sounded good. I could have been home ages ago. I've been on dozens of trucks that traveled close to home, but I always climbed into the next one and let it carry me away again. I'm a failure at that too, I guess.

And it brought me right to this moment in this fucking freezer.

I scoff and shake my head. This asshole is going to let me wallow in the downfalls of my life before I die. Dick.

My gaze turns toward the woman again, and something beneath her leg catches the light. I crawl closer and realize it's a bottle of whiskey. Since setting out on the road, I haven't really been a drinker anymore. It's not something I want to pick up again . . . but desperate times, right? I mean, if I'm staring death in the face, I might as well share a drink with the bastard.

"I'm sorry," I whisper to the woman before unscrewing the cap and swigging the chilled liquor.

The familiar burn races down my throat and hits my

stomach in a blaze of glory. Drinking may not be the answer to any of my many problems, but it sure as fuck is an answer to my pain. As I wait for the alcohol to work its magic, I scoot back to the wall—as far from the dead woman as possible—and drape the blanket over my head.

I take another sip as I shiver my life away. I drink until I feel warm from the inside out. At least something feels warm. And soon enough, I won't feel anything at all.

Chapter Twenty-Three

Jax

Every so often I'm thrust into the real world without much notice. There's a weird sense of panic as I find myself face to face with a situation I'm not aware of beforehand. I'm guessing Kane had a panic attack. Was it because of the girl?

Thinking of her and how she may have upset Kane sends a bolt of icy-fear through my sternum. I've been too complacent. I thought his deal with The Nameless would stop him from doing anything too drastic, but when it comes to Kane, drastic is his middle name.

"Aurora?" I call toward the back of the truck, but there's no response.

Pup whines and begins pacing between the front and rear of the truck. I dare to look back, unsure if I'll see her lifeless body, but I only see an empty cab.

What the fuck? Did she escape?

Or did Kane do something to her?

A sign for a rest stop pops up, and I nearly turn the

truck onto its side as I snatch the wheel and aim for the entrance. Once I bring the truck to a stop, I rush over to the bed and search for signs of a struggle.

The bed has been made, and nothing looks out of place. After pulling back the comforter, I examine every inch of the sheets for a droplet of blood or some indication of what happened. I find nothing. She's just . . . gone. It's as if she was never here in the first place.

I go to the sink next, and my eyes catch on a note stuck to the mirror.

I PUT THE BITCH IN THE TRAILER

Fuck. If she's in the trailer, odds are good that she's no longer alive. Kane likes to use the unit to keep his kills from stinking things up until he can find a safe place to dispose of them. My heart sinks.

"Goddamn it, Kane."

At least he was thoughtful enough to leave a note, I guess, but that does nothing for the pain I feel at the thought of losing her. While keeping her with us was a near guaranteed impossibility, the thought of her no longer existing in this world is almost more than I can stomach. She was special to me and Tobin. I hoped Kane would eventually see what we see in her, but I guess that was just wishful thinking.

I get out of the cab and walk toward the trailer. A cold sweat slicks my palms, and my brain refuses to accept what I'm about to see. And I don't want to see it. Even if she wasn't dead when he placed her back there, saving her is likely out of the question. I have no concept of time when I'm not in control, so that note could have been written an hour or a week ago.

After undoing the outer lock, I wrap my hand around the cold metal handle and close my eyes, steeling myself for what waits beyond the door. It opens with a clunk and a creak. I open my eyes.

"Aurora?" I yell into the freezer. I step inside the dark trailer and head toward the light at the end.

My gaze moves toward the body that I already knew about, then I allow myself to scan for the second one I hope isn't there. But there she is, curled against the wall with a blanket draped over her body.

I watch for signs of life, for the blanket to move up and down with each breath or for her head to turn as my feet clunk against the floor. She remains still, and panic clutches my heart in a vise. I care so much for that girl, even though I'm not allowed to. It's not fucking fair. And now she's gone.

"Oh, sweet girl," I say as I walk up to her frozen body beneath the blanket.

"I'm not dead," she whispers, but her voice is so low I almost don't hear it over the hum of the reefer unit.

I wrap my arms around her and tug her to her feet. The blanket falls away from her head, and the scent of alcohol smacks me in the face. I pick her up and carry her out of the truck and into the warm air. I rip the cold blanket away and take off my shirt so I can wrap it around her. Violent shivers tear through her body, so I draw her as close to my warmth as I can.

"I'm so sorry, sweet girl," I say. And I *am* sorry, even though I didn't do this. But I'm glad I was able to find her before . . .

I don't even want to think about it.

I carry her into the cab of the truck and flip on the bunk warmer as high as it can go. As I wrap her in every blanket I can find, my mind races through a labyrinth of confused thoughts. I don't know if Kane meant to kill her, but he came too close. He's done a lot of terrible shit to women, and he's often very creative with his slaughter skill set, but freezing a girl to death isn't anywhere near his typical MO.

Her teeth clack together, and the shivering hasn't slowed. She needs my warmth. I peel back the blankets and squeeze in beside her. Her head drops to my shoulder, and I let her cold body freeze mine so that she can take my heat. I'll give her all of me if it means she'll survive.

"What happened?" I ask.

"Kane's a fucking dick," she says through clattering teeth.

I stifle a laugh, glad to see her tenacity is still very much intact. "Fair. But why did he do this?"

"I don't know, Jax. One minute I was getting dressed, the next I was getting shoved into the freezer. He got an erection, but that's the only weird thing I can think of."

That would have enraged him, especially if she'd seen it, but I can't think about that right now. I'm just thankful she's alive and that I've been gifted this time with her. Even given the circumstances. Even knowing I can't keep her.

The sinking feeling returns and settles in my gut. She probably would have been better off if she'd died in that trailer. The Nameless will sell her to someone who will use and abuse her until she's no use to them anymore. She may think she's living through hell right now, but she's only standing outside the gates.

The worst part? There's absolutely nothing I can do about her future. I can't change Kane's mind. He nearly killed her just for giving him an erection.

Something clicks inside my mind.

If Kane wanted her dead, why did he write the note that told me where I could find her? If I hadn't seen the note, I would have kept driving and assumed the worst, and she would certainly have frozen to death.

In some weird way—a way Kane himself probably doesn't even realize—*he* saved her. His raw emotions were too powerful to contend with, so he shoved the danger into the freezer. Out of sight, out of mind. But he wrote the note and allowed me to take control, which means he didn't want her to die, even if that lack of want was subconscious.

But Kane is not unselfish. How could he do something from the kindness of his heart when his heart has no kindness? Has she affected him more than we realize?

I lift her chin and bring her eyes to mine. The icy pallor has begun to give way, allowing her cheeks to take on a pink hue. Better yet, the shivering has eased up. She still has a mild tremble to her lips as her jaw clenches and unclenches, but on the whole, she looks so much better.

I lean down and kiss her. She accepts my lips in ways I don't think I could if I was just in a freezer with a dead body. She's like no one we've ever met or anyone we'll ever meet again. She's a multi-faceted gem in a world of soot.

"Jax," she whispers against my lips. "Thank you for saving me."

I pull her into me and clutch her to my chest. "Are we going to talk about what you saw back there?"

"Can we not?" she asks. "Not right now, at least. There's a time and a place for discussions about dead bodies, but this isn't it."

I smile and brush back her damp hair. I wish so badly that he would let her inside him like we've let her in. Maybe he'd find something that could make him happy for once.

Being inside Kane is like living within an abstract painting. I'm surrounded by nonsensical shapes painted in blacks and grays and reds that represent his terrifying desires. I'd love for him to find some happiness so I don't have to feel so dreadful all the time too.

A sob works out of her chest, and I pull her tighter against me. Her tears don't fuel me the way they fuel Tobin or Kane. They destroy me. I never want to be the reason she cries. Technically, I'm not, but because we all share the same body, my hands placed her in that freezer.

"I'm so sorry," I whisper against her head.

"Don't let him out now," she says. "Please. I don't want him to see me cry."

I don't ask if she means Kane or Tobin, but I can only assume she means either of them. We each have our own set of skills, and comforting isn't something they're very good at.

"Do you want to talk about anything aside from what you saw in there?" I ask.

"Yes," she says through a fresh barrage of tears. "Why me?"

"You were just in the wrong diner at the wrong time."

"No, I'm not talking about getting kidnapped by you three. I mean, why did those men . . . ?" Her voice trails off, and she takes a deep breath. "If I tell you something, can the others hear me?"

I shake my head.

"There was a reason I left college, and it wasn't because I couldn't keep my grades up. I'd been at a party, but I got really drunk. Too drunk. When I stumbled back to my dorm room, I didn't realize someone had followed me home."

I already know where this story is going, and I don't like it.

"He was a young jock," she says. "A real party boy around campus. I guess I forgot to lock my door because one minute, I was ready to pass out on the bed, and the next, his hands were scalding every inch of my body. My tits. My ass. My thighs. I asked him to stop. I even tried to move away from him, but my arms and legs were like lead weights."

"Sweet girl, I'm so sorry."

"As fucked up as it sounds, I could have brushed it off if it had just been him. But he wasn't alone, Jax. I don't even know how many of his friends had tagged along, but it wasn't just him."

She buries her face in my chest and cries, and all I can do is hold her. I can't take her pain for her the way I can take Kane's pain. I can't lock her memories in a box so she can function. She has to do this on her own. All by herself.

For the first time, I realize just how lucky Kane, Tobin, and I are.

"It went on for hours," she finally says. "Sometimes I would pass out, only to wake up to someone else assaulting me. Jax, I bled for days."

"Did you report them?"

She shakes her head and sniffles. "I never went to the police because I felt guilty. I'd worn a short skirt and a halter top, and I won't pretend I hadn't flirted with the guy that followed me home."

Rage simmers beneath my skin. How can she blame herself? "It wasn't your fault. You have to understand that. Being flirtatious doesn't equal consent."

"That isn't how some men see it," she says with a bitter laugh. She takes another deep breath and lets it out. "You're the first person I've told. I've been too ashamed to tell anyone else."

I place my palm against her back and rub circles over the thin t-shirt. "You have nothing to be ashamed of. You are so incredibly strong, and I'm honored that you trusted me enough to share this with me."

She snuggles against me, wrapping her arms around my waist. "Can you hold me, Jax? Just for a little while. I know it can't be forever, but just hold me."

I lie back on the bed, pull her into me, and I hold her, all while my brain races with ways I can save her from the path of destruction we've placed her on.

Chapter Twenty-Four

Aurora

After shedding the weight of my secret, I'm so much lighter. I always thought telling someone would make me feel dirty or ashamed, but I feel neither of these things. Maybe I just needed the right person to talk to.

I wipe the lingering tears from my cheeks and revel in Jax's warmth behind me. It's difficult to lie beside a man who saved me from freezing to death in a refrigerated truck when he's stuck inside the body of the man who put me there, but I know they aren't the same. Jax doesn't want to harm me. He protects me in ways no one else has. As strange as it sounds, the same can be said for Tobin. Jax is my safe place to discuss my feelings, and Tobin is my safe place to explore my sexual desires without judgment.

Kane is the only danger.

Jax's arm drapes over my side, his hand resting on my stomach. Cuddling with Jax somehow feels so natural despite this completely unnatural situation. I don't know why he bothered to save me, though. I'm fairly certain I'll end up in that freezer again, especially after seeing the body back there. He can't stop Kane. I got lucky this time, but I've never been a lucky person. If it happens again, I'm fucked.

Pup jumps onto the bed and curls into a fluffy ball by Jax's hand. She whined incessantly when I first returned to the truck, almost as if she could sense just how close to death I'd come. Now that I'm warm and safe, she's content. I close my eyes and run my fingers through her soft fur.

Jax's hand rips away, and he scoots backward. Which means Jax is gone. And since he didn't grind on my ass when he woke up . . . that means he's Kane.

"Jesus fuck," he snarls, putting more space between us. "What the fuck!"

I turn over and try to control my widening eyes as I lock my gaze on him. "Jesus fuck what, Kane? I think I should be the one saying that. And what are you so afraid of? Thinking you're seeing a ghost?"

"I'm not fucking afraid," he says as he sits up.

I don't touch him, but I lean closer. "Your breathing is heavy. Your heart is racing. That's fear."

"I'm not afraid of *you*," he snaps as he goes to push me away, but I grab his wrist. Anger lights up his face. I expect him to hit me or rip out of my grasp, but he only freezes. He can't handle my touch. He's incapable of doing anything but sitting there and panting.

"You're afraid of something I represent," I say. "Do you hate women? *Whores*?"

"You don't know anything about me."

"I'm well aware, but whose fault is that? I know plenty about Jax and Tobin."

"Get your fucking hand off me." Even as he says this, he

still makes no effort to remove my hand. As big as he is, he'd only need to move his arm to snatch me loose.

Pup hops off the bed and begins pacing and whining. She stares at us with wide, glistening eyes. Her ears press against her head, and she begins to shiver.

"I'll let you go if you tell me why you put me in that trailer," I say.

He swallows and clenches his teeth. "Because you . . . Because I don't like how you affect us."

"Because I give those two the companionship they crave? Maybe if you let me, I could show you what it means to have a friend."

"I don't want that."

"I think you do. I think you desperately want to connect with another human being, but you're scared."

This breaks him from his frozen state. He throws me onto my back and raises his fist above my head. I don't flinch or cow to him, though. I just raise my chin higher because fuck him. I've nearly had a corpse party with a dead body in the freezer, so this is nothing.

He slams his fist down beside my head, and it sinks into the mattress. "Fuck you, dropout! The only reason I'm keeping you alive . . ."

I don't know what he's chosen to leave out, but I hope he meant to say he's kept me alive because of Jax and Tobin. Something deep inside tells me this is only wishful thinking. He's kept me alive for much more sinister reasons.

Kane leans over me, and his racing heart thumps against mine. "You mean nothing to me. You're lower than nothing. You're lower than the gum you chewed off my fucking shoe. I don't want companionship from you. I don't want *any*thing from you. The other two may see something in you, but I see nothing but a flunky whore."

His degrading words should make me recoil, but I play into the hulking mass of madness hovering over me and lift my head a fraction of an inch. His warm breath rolls over mine as I press my lips to his.

Shock and confusion flash across his face as he pulls back, but these emotions are quickly replaced by anger and something else. Embarrassment? Fear? I don't know. But his pupils dilate and instead of hitting me, I lose Kane in front of my eyes.

"You kissed the big, bad Kane, eighty?" He leans forward and bites my bottom lip. "Are you suicidal?"

I scoff. "He put me in the fucking trailer. I almost died."

"And that made you want to kiss him? You're even more fucked up than I thought." He smirks and rubs a hand down my chest. "Your sweet little lips traumatized him so much it forced a change neither of us expected. *Thrust* me right into your lap." He moves his hips against me to punctuate the word.

"I thought I could get through to him," I say with a shake of my head.

"No one has gotten through to Kane. No one." He gets off of me and sits on the edge of the bed.

"Has anyone gotten through to you before, Tobin?"

He offers me a sinner's smirk. "Nah. Just because I haven't connected with someone before you doesn't mean I couldn't, though. But him? He's physically and emotionally incapable."

"Challenge accepted."

He leans over, buries his hand in my hair, and cups my ear. "Don't be stupid, eighty. Just because you've gotten to me doesn't mean you'll get to him. Just drop it."

I wish I could. I wish I didn't care. But I can't and I do.

This desire to connect with Kane goes beyond wanting

to save my life. I've gotten close to Tobin and Jax, and while they're their own people, they're also part of Kane. I'm falling for them, and Kane is part of that package. Is it so bad to want him to want me?

Then a little voice pipes up in my head, reminding me that yes, it's pretty bad to want him to want me, especially after seeing that body in the trailer.

"Why does he kill women?" I ask.

A deep laugh rumbles inside Tobin's chest. "Because he hates them."

"I've figured out that much, Sherlock. But why? What happened to him?"

Tobin sobers now, the smile sliding from his face. "I've told you it's not anything you need to know. Why are you so stubborn?"

I grip his hand and look into his eyes. "Please, Tobin. Help me understand him."

He shakes his head and looks away. "He's been hurt pretty badly. He endured a lot of abuse from women who were supposed to protect him."

"Sexual abuse?"

"I shouldn't be telling you any of this."

"I understand him more than you realize," I say. "I was assaulted when I was in college."

I tell my story for the second time, and it hurts a little less than it did before. Tobin's jaw clenches and unclenches, and his eyes remain trained to the floor. When I finish, he looks up at me.

"You are so strong," he says, "but telling you what happened to Kane is a risk I can't take. That strong part of you is still embedded in who you are. Kane lacks that. That's where Jax and I come in. If Kane knew what happened to him, if he was forced to face it . . ."

"You're afraid I'll tell him and risk all of you?"

He blows out a breath. "I need a minute." He stands and walks to the front of the truck, then steps outside, leaving me on the bed.

It turns out Kane and I may have more in common than I thought, but I can't do anything with that information. Despite Tobin's fear, despite knowing that breaking Kane could save me in the end, I won't risk Jax or Tobin. Though I don't fully understand why, I'm unwilling to risk Kane as well.

A few minutes later, the driver's door opens and Tobin takes a seat behind the wheel. Or I think it's Tobin until he turns to me and says, "Buckle up, dropout. We have to take care of that body."

Chapter Twenty-Five

Kane

After checking my GPS, I spot a lonely stretch of road devoid of houses or farmland. Technology has become a double-edged sword; it sometimes catches men like me in a web, but it can also make finding remote areas a breeze. I turn out of the rest area and head toward the spot I've marked on the map.

The rear of the cab is quiet for once, which makes me uncomfortable. I've grown used to the girl's incessant talking, and the lack of that noise unnerves me now. I won't go so far as to say I enjoy it, but it's like running a box fan in your bedroom during the dead of winter. Sometimes the right kind of noise provides a bit of comfort, even if it adds to your discomfort in other ways.

I look over my shoulder and see her on the bed. Rather, I see her legs. The upper half of her body hides behind the partially outstretched curtain. Something about her body language makes my heart sore, and it's a feeling I neither like nor want to feel. Then I realize it's not my emotion. This is something Jax and Tobin feel.

Why?

It doesn't matter why, because you don't care about the whore.

Now I feel stupid for wishing I could hear her voice. It was never my wish to begin with. It's emotional bleed-through, which isn't something that happens very often for us. My inability to realize that—my inability to recognize their emotions as separate from my own—only shows just how damaged our compartments have become. Our ship is sinking, and the water has begun to breach our hull.

I have to get rid of this girl as soon as possible.

"Come on, dropout, let's bury that body," I say as I pull the truck to a stop. "I need to get the old girl cleaned before we pick up that load."

This body should have been buried several state lines ago. Pick up one, hold her until I kill her, bury her a state or two over. That's always been my plan. Taking Aurora fucked up everything, but I have to clean that trailer and provide proof to the distributor before I arrive to pick up the load. No one wants to put their perishables beside a dead fucking body.

I walk toward the back of the truck to retrieve the shovel I keep stashed beneath the bed. The girl hasn't moved. She continues to lie on top of the comforter, her hand lazily running through Pup's fur.

First she ropes in my alters, and now she's going for my dog. I can't with this bitch.

"You can dig one hole, or I can dig two. Your choice," I say. I'm not in the mood to argue with her.

"Why do I have to dig the grave?"

"Because I'm getting too old for this shit."

"Have you ever considered retiring?"

Retire from killing? Never.

My hand finds the shovel, and I pull it out and hold it toward her. "Get out there and dig, dropout."

She rolls her eyes and accepts the wooden handle, then stands up and plods out of the truck. When I step out behind her, I look at the sky and study the clouds as I draw a cigarette from the pack in my pocket. I lean against a tree and light it. Her eyes follow the cigarette as if it's a magic wand.

"What, do you want one?" I ask.

She nods.

"Beg me."

A scoff slips past her lips, and she tightens her grip on the shovel. "I'm not begging you for shit."

"Say, 'Daddy Kane, give me a cigarette because I'm a dropout whore who doesn't care about her body.'"

"*Daddy Kane* can suck my dick," she mumbles under her breath.

A smirk tugs at my lips. Even though her eyes hold so much longing for this little nicotine stick, she turns to head into the woods rather than play my game. I grip her arm and hand her my cigarette, and she looks up with a sneer before taking it from me. With an attitude like that, I'm amazed no one has beaten her to death before now.

I pull out another cigarette for myself and light both. She leans on the shovel and sucks in smoke with her eyes closed. I stare at her lips each time they wrap around the filter, and an uncomfortable feeling spreads through my body like poison.

I turn toward the truck. "I'm gonna let Pup out while we're stopped."

"You aren't worried she'll run off?" she asks as I open

the door. "I had a dog once, but he ran away when I took him on a hike. My dad wouldn't let me look for him because our trip was over and he wanted to get home. I don't want that to happen to Pup."

I whistle for the little dog, and she trots to the front of the truck and hops down. "I don't have to worry about Pup running off. We've been doing this for years, and she always sticks close."

Thunder rumbles in the distance, the sound carried on the darkening clouds creeping across the sky. Judging by the sharp, thick scent in the air, rain is on its way. We need to dig this grave and get back onto the road.

Aurora seems to sense the urgency as well, because she throws down her cigarette, snuffs out the cherry, then sinks the shovel into the dirt and pulls up a large clod of grass.

"What the fuck are you doing?" I ask.

"Digging a fucking grave?"

I shake my head and snatch the shovel from her hands. "You can't do it here at the side of the road. It'll be too obvious. We have to go into the woods a little ways."

"You want me to try to dig a grave in that?" She motions toward the forest. "I can't break through all those tree roots."

I wrap my hand around her bicep and drag her into the woods. "Ye of little faith," I mutter.

We walk for a few minutes, Pup scampering at our heels. When we come to a clearing, I push the shovel into her hands and raise an eyebrow. She scoffs and gets to work.

Aurora is much more methodical than I've ever been. I usually dig a hole that's just big enough to shove the body into and just deep enough to keep the wildlife away. She's really mapping this thing out. Using the shovel's blade, she's already drawn a rectangular perimeter. A very *large* rectangular perimeter.

"Are we burying a body or laying the groundwork for an in-ground pool?" I say. "What the fuck are you doing?"

She blows away a strand of hair that's fallen over her eyes. "I'm sorry. I seem to have misplaced my handbook on grave digging. Maybe an expert should show me how it's done?"

I shake my head as she holds the shovel out to me. "No, no. Carry on. It's just a little . . . big."

We could probably bury two bodies side by side in that thing, but I swallow a smile and go back to watching her dig. My eyes fall to the curve of her back. Sweat collects on the dip just above the waistband of her pants. Those soft lines tempt some buried emotion inside me, but I fight it off by imagining filling her mouth with that loose soil until she fucking suffocates. I have to think these thoughts to fight off the feeling that manifests into something deranged.

She wipes sweat from her forehead with the back of her hand when she's nearly halfway done. It leaves a streak of brown behind. Pup paces at the edge of the deepening rectangle, her little head lifting each time the thunder booms a bit closer. She's never been a fan of storms.

I open my mouth to tell Aurora I'm going to put Pup back in the truck, but lightning streaks across the sky and a loud boom swallows my voice. Before I know what's happening, Pup is a blur of brown as she disappears into the woods.

"Pup! No!" I scream, but it's too late. She's gone.

I look between the girl digging the grave and the woods. Leaving her would be stupid, but I can't lose my dog. My hand goes to my chest, my heart galloping against my palm at the thought of losing Pup. My jaw clenches. I'm not used to feeling sentimental feelings like this, but that dog means more to me than she should.

Memories rush back as I recall the way her little teeth sank into my hand as I tried to scoop up her battered body on the side of the road. By the time I carried her into the emergency vet, I was shaking as much as she was. I rented a room in a nearby motel so I could wait to hear if she'd pull through. It was the most human I'd ever felt. That little dog is my only tether to some form of humanity.

"Kane, you have to find her," Aurora says. "You go, and I'll keep digging."

It's a ploy. I'm not stupid. She sees an opening and she plans to take it. The moment I'm far enough away, she'll drop that shovel and disappear. I curse under my breath, torn in half by this decision.

Rain begins to patter onto my broad shoulders, and that makes up my mind. I have to go after my dog. She's too small to survive out here, especially in a storm, and the thought of leaving her behind does something terrible to me. I'll admit I'm attached to the fucking thing. And now she's gone.

"Don't go anywhere," I say, though I have to raise my voice to be heard over the sudden rush of wind tearing through the trees. "If it gets too bad out here, head back to the truck. Do you understand?"

She nods, but I don't believe her. I don't *trust* her. She's a woman, after all, and women have only shown me that they can't ever be trusted. Still, what choice do I have? I look at her for what I assume will be the final time, and then I head into the woods.

The rain falls in sheets now. The thick canopy holds most of it at first, only allowing intermittent drops to glide past the leaves and branches to land on me. Then the canopy can hold no more, and the torrent breaks through in a blinding wash of water. I call for Pup as I struggle through the thickening brush. I look for signs—fur left behind on a spindle of thorns or broken branches—but I see nothing.

Sharp twigs reach for me and scrape across my exposed skin. My voice is lost to a crescendo of rain, wind, and thunder. Lightning cracks nearby, too close for comfort, but I push on. I can't give up on my dog.

As I stumble along through the woods, I look for places where a small animal might seek shelter from this storm. I get on my knees and peer into every overhang, each rocky outcropping, but she isn't there. By the time the weather begins to let up, I'm soaked to the bone and completely hopeless.

I can't find her.

And I have to head back.

With a sigh, I turn around and begin picking my way toward the clearing. If I were capable of tears, I'd allow myself to cry right now. My exhausted body still clings to some frayed sliver of hope, though. Maybe the girl will still be there when I get back. Maybe my dog has returned. Maybe I don't have to be on my own again.

The sun sits low in the sky by the time I reach the clearing. I step toward the edge of the grave and peer into it. From the looks of things, she continued digging once I left, but she didn't hang around for very long. The shovel leans against the side of the empty hole. She's gone.

Maybe she just went to the truck.

Yeah, and maybe I'll wake up tomorrow with a million dollars and perfect mental health. The girl is gone. The dog is gone. And I have to accept it.

I grab the shovel and head to the truck. Even though I know I'll find the cab empty, I have to check. The storm finds renewed strength as I make my way through more branches and thorns, and another ten gallons of rain soak into my skin before I reach the desolate road. My fingers wrap around the door handle, and I haul myself inside.

I call out for the girl and Pup. Silence answers me. I check the cabinet above the bed and find her backpack tucked inside, but that doesn't mean anything. She didn't know where I'd hidden it, and she probably knew better than to come looking for it.

There's no point in stripping off my wet clothes. I still have to get rid of the body in the trailer. I still have to pick up a load in Texas. I still have to call The Nameless and tell them the deal is off.

Picking up my phone, I ready myself to dial their number, but then I stop. A text would work just as well, especially since I don't feel like hearing anyone's voice right now. I just want to be alone. Misery doesn't always love company.

I lost the package. Deal is off.

I recommend you find it. Money has already exchanged hands.

With a sigh, I shove my phone into my pocket and head into the rain again. I reach the back of the truck and lean my head against the rear doors. How did everything go so wrong? I never should have picked her up. If it weren't for Aurora, I wouldn't be in this mess. I would still have a dog, The Nameless wouldn't have scrawled my name on their shit list, and the dynamic between me and my alters wouldn't be so damaged.

I reach for the lock and begin to unfasten it when something stops me. A rustling in the bushes. Footsteps.

Turning toward the sound, I ready my hand over the knife attached to my belt, prepared to take out any threat. Then my hand falls to my side as Aurora emerges from the woods with my dog in her arms.

Chapter Twenty-Six

Aurora

I slide a dry shirt over my head and wrap a blanket around my shivering shoulders. Kane busies himself by toweling off the bedraggled ball of fur I rescued from the woods. It was stupid of me to look for the dog and come back. Even after I found Pup, I could have taken her and run, I could have escaped, but some invisible thread pulled me back here.

Well, two invisible threads, and their names are Tobin and Jax.

Having been confronted with an out and choosing to return has told me everything I need to know. Despite my inability to form a bond with Kane—and Kane's inability to form a bond with anything aside from the dog he now lovingly checks over for injuries—I have adhered myself to Tobin and Jax. I care about them, and I care about what happens to them. That's why I haven't pressed Kane about his sexual assault. Integration may be the goal for some people with DID, but it isn't their goal, and I want to respect that.

But how can any of this work?

To be in a relationship with them would mean tying myself to three people, one of whom can't stand me. I'd love to say the feeling is mutual, but my hatred for him has lessened as I've learned more about him from Jax and Tobin. He's a product of severe trauma, and it feels unfair to judge him so harshly now. There has to be some way to break through his walls.

Kane places Pup on the floor and pulls a worn ball from a cabinet. He tosses the ball across the truck, and Pup's paws clatter against the floor as she races to get to it. It slips beneath the bed, and she wedges herself into the small space, only emerging once she realizes she can't reach it. Kane eyes me as I kneel and dig beneath the bed to retrieve the ball as she whines beside me.

"Where did you find Pup?" I ask.

"I was cutting through a small town and saw her on the side of the road. She'd been hit by a car and left for dead."

"You saved her?"

"I guess."

I swallow hard. I always wondered why he had a dog at all, let alone a small, fluffy thing like Pup. I'm surprised he didn't run over her to finish her off instead of saving her. Something about this little dog has wormed into a heart he insists he doesn't have. If the dog could wiggle in there, I'm sure I can get inside too.

I go back up front and sit in the passenger seat. "Do you know why I dropped out of college, Kane?" I ask. Maybe we can connect if he realizes I've been through trauma too. We aren't so different—aside from the fact that I haven't taken to killing people for funsies.

"I don't care why you left college," he says without meeting my gaze. "We still have a body to bury, though. Once the rain lets up, we'll have to get it done."

I push ahead, ignoring his attempt to put me off. "I was assaulted. The pain and humiliation were too much, so I ran."

He swallows but says nothing.

"I know you don't give two shits about what happened to me, but it was pretty fucking traumatic. It shaped my life from that point forward. Brought me . . . Well, it brought me here."

He considers this, then says, "Why become a prostitute?"

"Why become a serial killer?"

A low laugh rattles his chest. "Fair."

"Do you remember what happened to you? Any of it?"

He shakes his head and picks at the side of his thumb. "Tobin holds that information for me in that fucked-up little mind of his."

"If you don't remember what happened, why do you have so much anger?"

His mouth opens and closes. Opens and closes. "I've given you enough about me, dropout. Let it go."

His soul is a door that opens just enough to give me a glimpse of his human side before slamming in my face again.

"We almost had a moment, Kane, you know that?"

He blows out a heavy breath. "I don't connect with people."

"Even after everything that's happened to me, I can still connect with people. I managed to connect with Tobin and—"

"Fucking Tobin isn't connecting. That fucker would connect with anything as long as there was a hole to use."

Now it's my turn to shake my head. "It might be difficult for you to understand, but I connect with both of your alters on very different levels. And not just in sexual ways."

He inhales a sharp breath. "Even if I could connect with someone, I wouldn't waste my time on someone like you."

Ouch. "Someone like me?"

"A whore," he says through gritted teeth, like it pains him to speak that word.

"I think someone's jealous."

He turns and grips the steering wheel. "I'm not fucking jealous."

"Your dick doesn't work. So what? Who fucking cares? I don't want your dick, if that's what you're worried about. I want to connect with you differently. Emotionally."

"Are you suicidal? It's like you want to die."

His words are a warning, but I've never been one to listen to warnings. I keep going.

"Who cares if you talk to me and tell me about yourself? You'll either kill me or let me go in the end, so who the fuck cares what secret parts of you I take with me?"

"You're literally insane. You know that, right? You have absolutely nothing to bargain with, yet you talk with your chest so high. A girl like you. You're too confident for your own good."

"Because I think we can help each other."

He laughs. "Help each other? Okay. Just sit there and shut your mouth. If I wanted to go to a shrink, I'd have abducted one of those instead of a whore."

This is pointless. I stand to go to the bed, but he grabs my hand.

"Meet me outside at the back of the truck. We still have a job to do."

"Yes, *Daddy Kane*," I say. I'm on a roll, clearly.

"That mouth is going to get you killed, dropout!" Kane yells as I open the door.

He's such an asshole. How did I ever think I could break through the multiple layers of steel he's put around himself?

The CB radio goes off as I climb out of the truck. I can't make out the voice coming through the speaker, but I hear Kane's response.

"This is Three Amigos. Everything's fine. Over and out."

Chapter Twenty-Seven

Kane

As she blindly follows me through the woods again, I'm overcome by a cloud of doubt. I can't deny I've begun to like having the dropout around. That much became clear when I thought she had run off. Instead of feeling glad, another emotion swirled inside me. An unfamiliar emotion. It was similar to how I felt when I thought I'd lost Pup.

I shift the frozen dead woman over my shoulder and duck beneath a low-hanging branch. She's heavy as hell. I don't remember her being this difficult to carry when I killed her. Then again, she wasn't an oddly positioned brick of human waste at that point. She'd been more malleable.

That's another layer to this problematic cake I've baked. I miss killing. It's not exactly a fun family activity, so I would have to give it up if I found a way to keep Aurora.

What the fuck am I thinking? I can't keep her. The Nameless have made that abundantly clear. Even so, I find my mind sifting through ways to get out of this. There has to be a way to cancel the arrangement with The Nameless. She saved Pup, for fuck's sake. I can't repay what she's done by handing her over to them.

But I can't save her.

You don't suddenly *change your mind* with The Nameless, not unless you want to be on the chopping block next. When I set everything in motion, I sealed her fate.

We approach the grave, but I avoid looking at Aurora. Despite all the shit I give her, she has helped me a bit. What have I done to help her? Jax and Tobin have put themselves out there for her. They've given her some form of the love she desperately craves. In a way, I guess we all crave that sort of love. Even me, though I won't admit that to anyone.

Maybe she was right. Actually, she was definitely right. I'm jealous of them and the affection she gives them. I can feel it inside me, like a slow spreading disease. It's a warmth I can't explain any other way. It was stupid of me to think she wouldn't worm into my heart when she wormed into theirs. We share the same fucking organ.

Unable to cope with my widening range of emotions, I drop the corpse-sicle beside the hole in the ground, and then I do what I do best. I make shit uncomfortable.

"Do me a favor, dropout. Lie in that grave."

She sighs and climbs inside, but she doesn't lie down. Instead, she resumes digging.

"Did I fucking stutter?" I ask. "The hole is plenty deep enough, and you made it more than wide enough, so there's no need to keep digging. Lie. Down."

Call it a trust exercise, but I want to see if she'll obey.

And she does. She sighs, tosses the shovel onto the level ground, and drops to her knees before lying back in the soil.

"Play dead," I say.

"What?"

"Did all that rain clog your ears? I hate repeating myself. Just do as I say."

"Whatever you say, *Daddy* Kane."

When she says my name like that, it does something to me. Something it definitely should *not* fucking do, and not just because it's uncomfortable for me. She doesn't realize she's playing with matches in a tinderbox.

Her eyes fixate and she lets her head loll to the side. Seeing her like that takes the discomfort to another level. I just wanted to fuck with her, but I've ended up torturing myself. I have to do something to stop this boulder from picking up speed and hurtling off a cliff.

I pick up the shovel, gather a clump of muddy soil on the blade, and throw it onto her face. She sputters and sits up. Her hands fly to her face as she tries to dislodge the grit from her mouth and eyes.

"Fucking dick!" she screams, spitting out soil as she sits up on her knees again. She stays that way, filthy and angry, and the sight of her in that position hardens me.

How is she having such an effect on me?

Pain knocks behind my eyes. It's Tobin. It has to be. I don't want to relinquish this time to him, but maybe it's best. It's the only way I can keep her safe.

For now.

Tobin

I RISE to the surface and eye the beautiful sight before me. Aurora is bent over, spitting and cursing as she tries to clean dirt from her face. I look at the scene around my feet—a massive grave, a body, a shovel—and put two and two together.

"A little dirty, eighty?"

"Oh god, not you," she says before spitting more dirt from her lips.

I hop into the grave and lean over her. "That's not a very nice welcome. Would you rather I let Kane play with you? His version of play is much less fun and a lot more murdery."

"You guys are fucking assholes."

"I never claimed to be anything else. Now turn around so I can bury your face in the dirt as I fuck you."

Her body tenses as I rip open my belt and unzip my jeans. There's a fire in her eyes, and I almost expect her to argue, but she doesn't. She nibbles her lip, thinking about the prospect of fucking in a grave beside a corpse, then turns around and looks at me over her shoulder as she positions herself on her hands and knees.

That's all the invitation I need. I drop to my knees and lower her leggings. I gather spit beneath my tongue and drip it onto the curve of her ass. A fistful of soil follows, and I spread the wet, gritty dirt along her skin.

"Such a dirty girl, eighty," I groan.

My hands race along her body, dipping beneath her shirt to grab her tits. Her nipples press against my palms, begging to be played with, but I have other plans first. I leave a trail of grit behind as my hand travels toward her hair. After lacing my fingers through the strands, I push her face into the soil. Her hands rake my thighs as I hold her against the ground, but she doesn't fight me.

When I let her up again, she gulps air. "A little warning would be nice," she says.

She doesn't tell me to stop, though. That's my girl.

Dried dirt coats her face, and my balls ache when I think of tears cutting a path through that dark layer. Eighty doesn't cry, though. If I want to make this happen, I'll have to push her body to an extreme to bring it out of her. With enough external stimuli, she'll weep.

I pull my belt from the loops, wrap it around her neck, and draw it tight. Her face reddens. Kane is going to be mad at me for marking up his product, but I want those tears to flow. I pull back my hand and slap her cheek. As her mouth opens and closes wordlessly, tears spill from the corners of her eyes. I keep releasing and tightening the belt until her cheeks are soaked.

"Good girl, eighty. Cry for me. You know how I like it."

I push inside her, and she clenches around me with every strangled breath. I hold the tail of the belt, intermittently choking her as I fuck her senseless. She can't even make a sound as her beautiful face reddens above the ligature. I want to hear her moans and whimpers, so I rip the belt from her neck. Her chest drops to the soil as she catches her breath.

"Dirty, filthy whore," I growl as I thrust deep inside her and hold it, savoring her warmth. I place my fingertips over her clit and rub her. "Such a good girl deserves to come, right?"

She nods as I lean down and bite her shoulder. I swirl my fingers around her and pound against her as I fuck her harder. She takes me so well.

Her hands drop to the soil and her fingers curl into the ground. She's getting close. I feel it. Who comes inside a grave? Both of us, I guess, because her impending orgasm is bringing me closer and closer to my own.

Aurora's body rushes forward as she tries to escape the

pressure of my cock. She gushes all over the earth and the front of my pants. What a way to christen a gravesite. This is a new one for me.

I pull back her hips and bury myself deeper again. Her walls pulse around me as she comes down from her orgasm. I pull out of her and spill my come on her filthy, muddy flesh. When I'm finished, I push her forward and lick her clean. Earth and sweat glide across my tongue, mixing into a gritty symphony, but I'm not done yet. I fist her hair and lick her fucking tears, adding a bite of salt to the mixture in my mouth. Then I spread her lips, spit the dirt-coated come into her mouth, and follow up by pushing my muddy fingers to the back of her throat.

I stand and circle her, staring at her face. "You're so dirty. Filthy fucking whore."

My hand winds through her hair. My other hand pushes my jeans down my thighs. She lifts her body as if she's preparing to suck my dick, but that's not what I want her to do. Instead, I keep my hand wrapped up in her hair and turn away from her. I lean over the lip of the grave and spread my legs a bit. With a smirk on my face, I drag her toward my ass and bury her face between my cheeks.

"Eat my ass, eighty. Bury that dirty fucking face and eat me like I ate you."

I expect her to fight me, but she leans in. Her tongue slips from her mouth and grazes my asshole, and my fingers sink into the soil. Pleasure rips through me as she tongue-fucks me. With each movement of her warm mouth, I harden more because she's pleasing me in a way so few have.

God, I love this girl.

I wrap my hand around my aching cock and stroke, bathing in the intensity of the sensations behind me. The sounds, the feeling—it's all fucking euphoric. She's sloppy about it too, and that makes me want to fill her filthy mouth. I let her lick me until I'm close, then I rip her away from me and pivot toward her.

"Open your mouth," I command.

She spreads her lips, and I stroke the head of my cock against the tongue that worked me up to this moment. I fill her mouth, grip her hair, lean her back, and spit on her waiting tongue.

"Swallow." I watch her throat as she swallows all of what I've given her. "I love what you do to me, eighty."

She sits back on her ass, eyes wide as she stares up at me. She knows that's as close as I'll come to saying I love her, but the meaning is the same. Somehow, some way, Jax and I have to save her.

Chapter Twenty-Eight

Kane

I'm back behind the wheel of the truck. We've reached Arkansas, which means Tobin or Jax have been with her for a while. I can only assume they eventually dumped the body in the grave. There's no way I'll ask her about it. Not when she looks so satisfied. Like a cat with a saucer of milk, she just sits there with a smile on her face as she stares out the window. Her hand drags lazy strokes through Pup's fur.

Tobin. Jax. Pup. They all adore her. How will they feel about me after I sell her?

I shift in my seat and tighten my grip on the wheel. There's something genuinely wrong with me and I'm surprised I can even recognize the doubtful feelings inside. I just know that it's nagging me to the point of discomfort.

She looks over at me, and the smile drops from her face.

"Hey, Kane," she says.

A feeling stirs inside me, deep within the crater that

once housed a heart. She recognizes each of us. She doesn't think we're crazy for having three minds in one body. Instead of being a judgmental asshole, she acknowledges our differences and our situation. Instead of calling us names or accusing us of fabricating what we can't even control, she accepts us as we are.

Well, she accepts Jax and Tobin. She still doesn't care for the things that make me who I am. Or the lack of the things I could never be.

A sign for a truck stop looms in the distance. My bladder could use a little relief, so I turn in. As I pull the truck to a stop, I eye the girl. She must have used a rag to wipe the dirt from her face, but her nails are still filthy. She'd probably appreciate a shower.

"I'm gonna stop here for a piss break and some food. Can I trust you to shower without running off?" I ask.

"I would love to shower, but how the fuck am I supposed to pay for it? You stashed my wallet, along with the rest of my shit."

I ease my wallet from my back pocket and pull out a twenty. Her eyes light up as she reaches for it, but I pull it away before her fingertips can so much as graze the paper.

"Not so fast," I say. "If you try anything, if you so much as *think* of—"

"You'll break my neck or put me in the freezer or both. Got it." She leans forward and takes the money without batting an eye at my implied threat. "Besides, you don't have to worry about me running off anymore. You might be more intolerable than a Kathy Griffin marathon, but I actually like hanging out with Jax and Tobin."

With a smug smirk, she opens the door and exits the truck, leaving me with another mess of confused feelings. Knowing she prefers them to me is beginning to sting.

I stand and stretch my legs before walking to the back of the truck. A magazine rests on the bed, which is odd. It's a vintage *Playboy*—one of Tobin's prized possessions. I sure as fuck don't have any use for it, and I doubt Jax would know what to do with it. He'd probably whine about it being so degrading to the women.

Picking it up, I look at the woman on the cover. She's attractive, but she's also heavily photoshopped, and her tits are lopsided. I laugh and shake my head. Only I would notice the asymmetry instead of getting a boner.

As I go to return the magazine to Tobin's cupboard of pornographic wonderment, a slip of paper falls from inside. I bend down and pick it up.

KANE,
IF YOU HURT ONE HAIR ON THAT GIRL'S HEAD,
YOU'LL DESTROY ALL OF US, INCLUDING YOURSELF.
CALL OFF THE DEAL AND SAVE HER. IF WE CAN'T
KEEP HER, TAKE HER HOME.
-TOBIN

I crumple the note and shove it into my pocket. Against everything I am, I want to save her too. I just have to find a way to satisfy The Nameless. If I can find another girl as beautiful and clean as she is, that might be the answer to all of my problems, but the odds aren't in my favor. They're expecting a girl in the next twenty-four hours. It would take time to source another one.

It's not like I can pull just any girl off the street. I have to play by the same rules I use when choosing a victim. No family. Unwanted. Someone who won't be missed. I walk to the front of the vehicle and look at the parking area for the trucks. One lonely lot lizard crawls across the heated pavement, but she's too used up to serve my purpose.

I've never felt so conflicted in my life.

"Stay put," I say to Pup as I exit the truck. After I get this pressure off my bladder, I might be able to think more clearly.

A blast of cold air and gospel music rushes toward me as I enter through the truck stop's glass doors. A teenage boy sits behind the singular register. He's too busy scrolling on his cell phone to look up and acknowledge me. I walk past him and head for the restroom to the nauseating country rendition of "Amazing Grace."

After relieving myself and buying a few bags of chips and a couple of sodas, I head back to the truck. I'll wait for the dropout before I head into the diner. She's probably famished. Digging a grave is hungry work, and if anyone would know that, it's me.

If I hadn't taken her, I'd be as happy and murdery as always. Now I'm miserable because she's upended everything. Jax and Tobin may have benefited, but I sure as shit haven't, and getting some kind of drive to be around her only hurts me because she'd rather be around anyone else. Women have caused enough hurt in my life, and I'm not exactly eager to experience more of it.

I open the driver's side door and climb inside. Pup is busy pacing back and forth, a low whine shivering out of her with every few steps she takes on her three tiny paws. She does this if I'm gone for too long, but she usually stops once I'm back in the truck. This time, she just keeps pacing and whining.

I pat my leg, and Pup hops into my lap. "No need to worry. She'll be back," I say as I stroke her head. Do I say this to reassure the dog . . . or myself?

I'm not sure.

If I were her, I'd have taken this golden ticket and hopped on the first train to pull into the station. I just made her bury a body, for fuck's sake. And that was *after* locking her in the freezer and treating her like absolute dog shit for days on end. I really didn't think this through.

I look at the time on the dash clock. She's been gone for almost twenty minutes now. That's more than enough time to shower and throw on some clothes. I'm about to head inside and beat down a shower door when my phone buzzes in my pocket. I pull it out, and my chest immediately tightens. It's a text from The Nameless.

Did you find the girl?

No, not yet.

The lie rolls so easily from my fingertips. Too easily. These men hold too much power for me to deceive them like this.

Are you sure about that, Three Amigos?

My mouth goes dry. I've never told them my CB handle. I thought it was a little odd that someone radioed yesterday while we were preparing to bury that body, but I chalked it up to a trucker being nosy about why a reefer unit was turning off at a heavily forested area. Now?

Now I think I need to get the fuck out of here.

I'm about to get out of my truck to find Aurora when my phone vibrates again. Instead of a text message, it's a picture that sends ice barreling through my veins. The image is a bit blurry, but I can make out the duct tape wrapped around the girl's head and the zip ties binding her wrists together in the leather-clad backseat of a sedan.

The Nameless have Aurora.

Chapter Twenty-Nine

Aurora

I never even made it into the truck stop. Just as I reached the door, a man approached me, stuck a gun into my side, and guided me toward a dark car. After taping my head and securing my wrists, we pulled out of the parking lot. The last I saw of Kane, he was exiting his truck. I only hope he'll realize I've gone missing and that I didn't leave of my own free will.

The sun set hours ago, but the car continues down the interstate on a nightmare trip that seems never ending. We crossed into Texas a while back, putting more distance between me and any hope of rescue. I've loosened the duct tape around my mouth by licking the adhesive. I can't do shit about the zip ties biting into my wrists.

Using my tongue and chin, I lower the duct tape and clear my throat. "Can someone please tell me why I'm being kidnapped . . . again?"

The man in the passenger seat turns to face me. "We are simply taking possession of what belongs to us."

A hint of an accent colors each word in a diluted hue of Russian, but that isn't what my brain latches onto. "What belongs to you? I don't belong to anyone."

I expect a retort, a snide comment or an angry brush off, but he simply laughs and faces the front again. I pull back my leg and kick his seat.

That gets his attention.

He turns to face me again, and the anger in his eyes does more to satisfy than scare me. "You little bitch. If you know what's good for you, you'll remember that your legs are meant for spreading, not kicking."

I've never been one to know what's good for me, so I kick his seat again. "Tell me what the fuck is going on!"

He says something in Russian, and the driver pulls the car to the side of the road. Something silver glints in his hand, and then the barrel of a gun levels on my head. "You will shut the fuck up or I will shut you up. Someone paid a very high price for what you have between your legs, and I would hate to lose that money because I had to kill you. If you have a complaint, take it up with Kane. He made the deal." He laughs again as he faces the front. "Not that you will ever see him again."

I do shut up, but not because of the gun in his hand or the threat he made. Not even because he said I'll never see Kane again. I shut up because I can't breathe.

Kane . . . sold me?

He isn't exactly a candidate for an upstanding citizen award, but I never imagined he would do something so horrible. Choke me half to death and stick me in a freezer? Sure. Force me to dig a grave for a woman he murdered? Understandable. But this? It's more than I can take.

I stare out the window as the sedan lurches onto the road again. Trying to catch the attention of passing cars isn't an option. The windows are tinted to hell and back. For the first time in my life, I don't see a way out. I've always been good at running, but now there's nowhere to run. Kane sold me to these men, and they've turned around and sold me to someone else.

"How much?" I ask.

The man turns toward me and raises an eyebrow.

"How much did you pay him?" I clarify.

"For you?" A hellish smile eases onto his face. "He sold you for a partial repayment of his debt to us. The amount is not important."

A sign slides by on the side of the road, and I realize we're nearing Houston. My brain flicks back to the inspection when Jax took control. Didn't he say they had to pick up a load in Texas? Does that mean all three of them were in on this?

My stomach sinks, and if it drops any lower, it will probably fall out of my asshole. If they were all privy to this plan, that means I was used by all of them. *Deceived* by all of them. The men I've been falling for have planned to get rid of me all along, and my heart and vagina were too blinded by need to see it.

I close my eyes and rest my head against the leather. The car turns onto a side road, but I don't look to see where we are or where we're going. What's the point? I have no control. I can't change the ever downward-trending trajectory of my life.

After a few more turns and bumping along a road that's more pothole than asphalt, we pull up at a large house in a small neighborhood. Or what might have been a neighborhood at one time. Now there is only one house on the street. The others have been reduced to weed-ridden foundations.

The men exit the car and come to my door. As they haul

me away from the leather interior, I'm surprised by how gentle they are. Their fingers don't dig into my arms. They don't push or hit me. Like guiding a dumbfounded sheep to the slaughter pen, they just move me along with the threat of a gun.

Once we're inside the house, they remove the duct tape from my head and the zip ties from my wrists before looking me over like two pickers examining a grandfather clock at an antique mall. They study my flaws, pointing at the red marks on my wrists and the bruises on my throat as they mutter to each other in a language I can't understand. Then, in clear English, the shorter one tells me to strip.

"Absolutely not," I say, crossing my arms over my chest.

He pulls out the silver pistol and waves a reminder at my head.

I don't move. Maybe it wouldn't be so bad to die. A few moments of pain, and then it will all be over. But the slimmest hope of escaping this mess won't allow me to give up. Damn my drive to survive.

Gripping the hem of my shirt, I close my eyes. I've taken off my clothes for countless men, but something about this situation makes me feel almost shy. Almost dirty. The choice and control have been taken from me, much as it was when I was in my dorm room. Tears gather behind my clenched lids, but I won't let them fall. Tobin will be the last man to have seen me cry.

"Hurry up. We don't want a striptease," the taller man says. "We're simply inspecting the merchandise."

Both men laugh, and the sound makes my skin crawl. I strip off the rest of my clothes so they can walk around and examine me. And they do. They raise my arms, lift my breasts, and spend far too long discussing my ass. When they've finished, they motion for me to dress again. I can't put my clothes on fast enough.

I'm led to a door in the kitchen and ushered down a narrow flight of stairs that drops into darkness. The door closes behind me, followed by the sound of a heavy chain locking me inside. A light clicks on above me seconds later.

I glance around the concrete-lined space. A stained mattress lies on the floor, and they haven't even bothered to offer any sheets. I hope they aren't expecting a five-star Yelp review from me.

I don't let my gaze linger on the stains, choosing instead to focus on the narrow table against another wall. A sandwich wrapped in plastic film sits on top of it. I remove the plastic, fully expecting to find two slices of bread and a piece of cheese, but I'm partially wrong. They've included a glob of mayo and a few slices of what smells like salami. A plastic cup with lukewarm water stands beside it.

If they think I'm eating this shit, they're delusional. I suppose I'm a little delusional as well, because I can only think of how much I miss the gas station food Kane keeps hidden around his truck.

I can only think of how much I miss *them*.

After tossing the sandwich onto the table, I sit on the floor and pull my knees to my chest. No one is here to see me cry, so I let the tears fall. How did I ever think I could get through to Kane? I was starting to see something in him that wasn't even there. Jax and Tobin fooled me first, though. Being in a relationship with three men is all fun and games until all of them betray you and break your heart.

I will never forgive them for what they've done.

Chapter Thirty

Kane

It's well after midnight as I pull my truck into a parking spot at a truck stop just outside of Houston. Pup sits on the seat beside me and whines. She hasn't let up since Arkansas, and the constant sound only adds to my headache.

"What do you want from me? She's gone," I say as I stroke her fur and try to settle her.

What do any of them want from me? We couldn't keep her. She has *never* been something we could keep. Tobin and Jax knew that from the beginning. We've always had two options, and those were killing her or selling her to The Nameless. The choice was made for me, and now we just have to accept it. That's why I'm heading straight to pick up the load in Houston. I have to let things return to normal.

Well, I want them to return to *my* version of normal, and I can start by checking out my prospects in the parking lot.

Nothing cheers me up more than taking a life, so I eye

the women floating between the trucks like bugs drawn to light. Ugly bugs, with pock-marked skin from drug-induced flesh picking and eyes as dull as their greasy, unkempt hair. A blonde looks over and smiles at me. The three or four teeth still clinging to her red gums have more tenacity than the tank man of Tiananmen Square.

I stand and go to the back of the cab before she has a chance to come any closer. I'm drawn to the cabinet where I hid Aurora's backpack. After pulling it from its hiding place, I sit on the bed. I remember going through it and finding her old college ID. Her auburn hair was pulled into a high ponytail, and she had such a sweet, genuine smile on her face (which also included a full set of healthy teeth).

That smile is probably very gone now.

I remember her telling me about why she quit school. I may not have seemed like I was listening, but every word came through in painful clarity. She didn't deserve what happened to her then, and she doesn't deserve what's happening to her now.

Despite my half-assed attempts to lie to myself, the truth won't be denied. I didn't drive through the night to reach Houston because of the product I need to pick up. I came to save the girl.

I drop the backpack on the bed, rush to the driver's seat, and start my truck. After spending my entire life only thinking about myself, I'm thinking of someone else now. Pup must sense my heroic shift, because she stops whining and finally settles on the seat.

Even if I die in the process—which is highly likely—I can't let any more harm come to Aurora. Maybe I can talk to them. Maybe I can negotiate a higher interest rate in exchange for her life. Then I scoff because there's no way they'll talk to me about her. When I head into their territory, we're all as good as dead.

I put my truck in drive and head toward the one place I never wanted to go back to: my old neighborhood.

The Nameless have a warehouse, but I doubt they've taken her there. They like to keep the product at their house on my old street. The soundproof basement is the perfect holding pen.

I shudder when I think of Aurora down there.

When I've gone as far as I can go in the truck, I pull into an overnight parking lot and grab my pistols from the lockbox. I stuff one down the back of my pants and cover it with my jacket and latch the other around my ankle. The cuff of my jeans conceals it. Strapped and ready to go, I give Pup what is likely a final scratch behind the ears and tell her to guard the truck.

The little dog looks up at me expectantly. She doesn't realize this may be the last time she ever sees me.

I exit the truck and head toward the neighborhood I grew to hate. There were only three houses on the long, quiet road. No one heard me screaming as a child. Or if they did, they just didn't care. The Nameless lived on the end. I'm really hoping our longstanding acquaintance leverages things in my favor, even though I hardly know anything about them now.

After several blocks, I'm standing at the start of the street that haunts my nightmares. I try to avoid looking at my childhood home, but my gaze pulls toward it. It's just a slab of concrete now, which is probably for the best. I can only recall brief glimpses of the last time I was in that house.

I only know that I murdered my stepmother in a fit of blind rage.

I'd stopped by to see my father, but she had answered the door. She tried to hug me, and I ended up choking the life from her body. Why? I don't know, and I don't want to know.

I lit the house on fire on the way out. Incredibly, I was never caught, but I ended up in prison a few years later after I got drunk and tried to grab some bitch outside of a bar. I never even got her back to my truck. If I had, I would've gotten away with it. I learned my lesson then. Stay away from booze and always get them in the truck first.

I continue toward the house at the end of the street without giving the crumbling foundation a second glance. The corpses of those secrets deserve to stay buried.

I creep to the edge of a window on the side of the house and peer inside. The bedroom is empty, but the open door gives me a straight view into the hallway. Ivan, one of the brothers, stands in the doorway. I see no need to keep them nameless any longer. They've lost their hold on me.

Grass rustles against my boots as I make my way into the backyard. Peering into another window, I see one of the brothers seated at the kitchen table. I can't make out which one, but it doesn't matter. They'll all be dead by dawn.

I'd like to avoid using the pistols if I can. Even though this is the only house left on this street, there are other nearby streets that are likely still very much inhabited, and nothing makes a noise quite like a gunshot. Though I imagine if Victor has been operating here for the last decade or more, there has already been a gunshot or two.

I don't love killing with a pistol, though, and that's another reason I'd rather use my knife. Guns are so impersonal. I'd much rather kill up close and feel their life force leave them. There's something almost serene when someone dies in front of you, and it's even more intoxicating when they die *because* of you.

I haven't changed my stance on murdering women, despite my current situation. Hell, I even still view the girl as killable. But something about her also makes me want to snatch her back and keep her for myself. Well, myself and Jax and Tobin. I swear they're driving my decision to rescue her because this is highly unlike me.

Weighing things out in my head only confuses me further. I could walk away right now and find a girl I could actually kill, or I could rescue one I can't ever kill. The scale leans toward the former, yet here I am.

Jax knocks against my skull as I stand behind the back door. I can't let him out. Not now. He'll only get himself killed by trying to talk his way out of this situation, and that's why I need to stay in control. I can do what needs to be done.

Ivan enters the kitchen, and I duck below the windowsill so he can't see me as I strain to hear their conversation.

"Sacha, where's Vic?" he asks.

"Down in the basement with the girl. You should probably get down there before he does something stupid."

"Or I could go down there and help him do something stupid," Ivan answers, and both men burst into a fit of booming laughter.

"Yeah, go down. I'll join you two shortly."

Ivan's footsteps fade away, and I dare to peek through the window again. I need to make a move soon, before they have a chance to hurt her.

Sacha stands and moves toward the fridge. He opens it and begins digging around. This is my opportunity to eliminate one of them, so I ease the back door open and step inside. He must hear me behind him, because his body tenses and he stands upright.

Before he has a chance to call for his brothers, I wrap my hand around his mouth and drag my knife across his throat. The blade pierces his flesh and the blood pours. The metallic scent sends me into a frenzy. It's like a high I can't explain. I hold the man against my chest until he stops flailing. Then I drop him beside the island, grab the beer bottle he pulled from the fridge, and pop it open. I pour it into my mouth, careful not to let my lips touch the rim.

One down, three to go.

It's hard for me to stay controlled now, with the scent of blood following me through the kitchen. The stuff is potent. I set the beer on the counter and make my way to the basement door.

Pulling the gun from my waistband, I open the door and start down the stairs. Each step sends a loud creak into the air.

"Hurry down, Sacha," Victor calls. "The fun is just beginning."

As I reach the bottom of the stairs, the men don't turn to face me. They expect their brother to join them, but they're in for a big surprise. Aurora sits on Ivan's lap. He's stroking her hair, and she keeps batting his hand away with an annoyance I've grown to like.

Maybe I'm doing this because I actually respect that girl. She's been so stoic and unbreakable since I've taken her, and that has to come from a place of immense inner strength. Breaking her became a challenge for me, but she never stopped being a snarky bitch, even in the face of death. And she hasn't changed. In an unknown place, with unknown men, she's still being bitchy. That takes a certain kind of bravery—or stupidity.

"Who's going to test her out first?" Victor asks. His back faces me, but each word reaches me as if I'm standing right beside him.

My blood begins to boil in my veins. A strong sense of possession overcomes me, but I can't tell if this feeling is mine. Even if it's from Tobin or Jax, I still feel the raging fire in my body.

Right now, none of that matters. Regardless of whose emotions I feel, Ivan's hands on her body are making me absolutely homicidal.

I fight the toxic thoughts swirling in my mind about her —a misdirected barrage of repressed trauma. I silence the voice that says she deserves to be in this place because of who she was before I took her. I rein in the thoughts that encourage me to walk out now, and I take a step forward.

As my broad frame comes into the light, Victor turns to face me. I revel in the shock coloring his pale face. "Kane, what the hell are you doing?" he asks.

"I made a mistake," I say, "and I've come to fix it."

Ivan makes a move for a gun sitting on a nearby shelf, but I raise my pistol and aim at him before he gets more than a few steps. He freezes. My truth is written on my face. If they move a fucking muscle, I'll shoot.

"Hey, dropout. Be a peach and restrain Victor." I nod toward a roll of duct tape on a wooden table.

"Fuck you, Kane," she says.

My eyes widen. "Would you rather hang out with them? Because I could leave."

She scoffs and climbs off Ivan's lap. He tries to hang on to her, probably to use her as a human shield, but she thrashes her heel against his shin until he lets go. She grabs the tape from the table and heads toward Victor, who sneers at her before putting his hands behind his back.

With a wide grin, she begins winding the tape around his wrists.

"You're dead, Kane," Ivan says from the chair.

"Tape Ivan too," I say to Aurora, gesturing toward the man with my chin. "And cover his mouth."

When Victor's hands are secured, I step closer to him. He has to look up at me because he's considerably shorter.

"How did you find me?" I whisper.

"Do you think we would be stupid enough to allow you to drive into the sunset with something we purchased before it was paid off? I installed a tracker beneath the driver's step."

I nod and step away from him.

Once she's finished one hell of a tape job, I walk over to Ivan, pocket my pistol, and draw my knife. Gripping his dark hair, I crane his neck and ignore his muffled pleas as I sink the blade into his throat. I begin twisting the handle, and I don't stop until a spray of blood jets across all of us.

"No!" Victor screams. "We've always been good to you, you fucking bastard!"

Unfortunately, that's true, and I'm destroying our little arrangement to save the girl. The one who's looking at me with complete hatred.

I walk up to Victor, a smile on my face because I'm fully intoxicated by all the blood at this point. I tighten my grip on my knife and, with a quick motion, I jab it in the soft space beneath his chin. Blood fills his mouth, and judging by the way he struggles to speak, I can only assume I pushed hard enough to spear his tongue as well. He drops to the floor and begins writhing around.

I thought I had eliminated the risk until a solid punch wrecks my jaw. I shake my head and turn toward Aurora.

She's clutching her fist because she really used all her effort to hit me. I push her against the wall.

"Don't ever fucking hit me, dropout."

"I have the right to be mad. You fucking sold me! You asshole!"

"I got you back, didn't I?"

"Fuck you!" she screams.

"We'll talk about this later. Right now, I need to finish this."

I step closer to Victor, jab the knife into his neck, then use my boot to put pressure on the handle until the blade's tip hits the concrete floor. Blood pours from his mouth, and the jerking turns to twitching before he finally stills.

I turn to Aurora and hold out my hand. "Let's get out of here."

She sets her jaw and balls her hands into tight fists at her sides. "I'm not going anywhere with you."

Chapter Thirty-One

Aurora

My chest rises and falls with a blast of panicked anger. A ribbon of blood stands stark across my chest, but it's nothing compared to the river of red washing over Kane. He's covered in the stuff. He takes a step toward me and reaches for my hand, but I pull away. The look of hurt on his face almost makes me want to comfort him, but then I remember what he's done to me.

"Why, Kane?" That's all I can manage to say.

He runs his hand through his hair and shakes his head. "I'll explain everything, but we can't hang around a fucking crime scene. We need to get out of here."

"I'm not going anywhere until you give me a good reason for fucking *selling me*!"

He grabs his knife from Victor's throat and tucks it into his waistband. Then he comes toward me. Before I know what's happening, he's hoisted me over his shoulder and started up the stairs. I pound against his back, but it's like hitting a brick wall. I'm the only one getting hurt. I stop pounding and go limp as we pass another dead body and exit the house through the kitchen.

Once we're outside, he sets me on my feet. "We're covered in blood. We can't wash up here, so we'll have to be careful as we move back to the truck. If anyone sees us—"

"Us? We? What part of what I said didn't make it through your thick skull? Our fun little road trip ended as soon as you decided to sell me to the highest fucking bidder!"

He rushes toward me, turns me around, and pulls me against his chest with his hand over my mouth. "Keep your fucking voice down. I promise I'll take you back to your home in New York, but I want you to hear me out first. Your other option is to beg for a ride somewhere else, and I can guarantee no one is going to help you when you've got someone's blood all over you."

He makes a good point.

I relax in his arms, and he releases me. We spend the next thirty minutes cutting a path through overgrown backyards attached to what appear to be abandoned houses. He chooses our route carefully, analyzing the way forward before taking a step in any direction. We're both winded by the time we reach the truck. He bends near the step beside the driver's side door, fishes around beneath the metal, and pulls a small black box from underneath. He tosses it into the bushes and opens the door. The sun begins to rise as we climb inside.

Kane tosses a rag to me, and we begin cleaning the blood from our skin as Pup scampers around our feet. I don't reach down to pat her until I'm all clean and dressed in a change of clothes.

I sit on the bed and wait for the explanation I'm owed. It doesn't matter in the long run, I guess. I've made up my mind, and I want nothing more to do with any of them. But curiosity gets the better of me, and I want to hear what he has to say, even if it won't change anything.

When he's all clean, he comes and sits beside me on the bed. "I won't deny that I sold you. That part is true. But I tried to call off the deal."

"You didn't try very hard."

"Why do you think they had to come and kidnap you?"

I don't have a good answer for that.

"Exactly. I told them I no longer had the package—you—but they wouldn't listen. They were tracking me."

I turn to face him now. "Did Jax and Tobin know?"

He nods. "They knew, but they couldn't stop it. They have a duty to protect me, and that meant they couldn't do anything that would potentially get me killed. They have autonomy and can make their own choices, but it only goes so far."

"So why did you come for me?" I ask the question even though I'm afraid of the answer.

"For Jax and Tobin."

"Not for yourself?"

He stands and begins pacing. "I don't know, dropout. I'm not exactly fond of you."

For the first time, I see just how difficult it is for this man to discuss his feelings. It's not a matter of want. It's an impossibility.

Kane stops pacing and begins rubbing his eyes. I've seen him do this before when Tobin or Jax try to come through. They're trying to protect him. From what? Feelings?

Despite everything he's done, I can't stop my heart from aching at the sight of his struggle. And even though I want to continue being mad at him—at all of them—I can't. He said he tried to stop the deal, and I believe him. He came after me. He saved me. Now I need to help him.

"Kane, come sit down," I say. "We don't have to talk about anything else if you don't want to. I . . . believe you." Fuck, that was hard to admit, but I have to do what's best for him right now.

"No, you don't understand," he mumbles. "And no matter how much I want to make you understand, I can't, because I don't even understand. I live with so much anger inside me, and I don't even know why. I only know that I don't want to know more. Do you know what that's like? Do you have any idea?"

I shake my head because no, I don't understand. I can't. But I want to.

On shaking legs, I stand and go to him. It's a risky move. He'll probably turn around and beat me to death with his fists, but I have to try. I have to connect with him, and nothing is more powerful than touch. People connect on so many levels, but touch is universal.

It's also the one thing that sends Kane over the edge.

Swallowing my fear, I step closer and wrap my arms around him. My cheek presses against his warm back, and I just hold him. I shove the lingering animosity into my gut, and I close my eyes as I mentally beg him to accept me.

His body relaxes in my arms, and his hand closes over mine. As his breathing begins to slow, I think I've finally gotten through to him. Then he turns and clamps his hand around my throat.

Chapter Thirty-Two

Kane

My panic stems from never having the clear picture of what makes my body respond like this. I feel and see bits and pieces of something I never truly understand, and it causes a rage to grow until it overflows. That's why my hand is around her throat. That's why I'm squeezing.

A blinding pain pierces my head, and for the first time, memories rush to me. Crystal clear. Painfully clear. In an attempt to stop me from strangling Aurora, Tobin opened the box and let my demons loose, and I can see everything my stepmother and her sister did to me.

The touching.

The *fucking*.

The outright abuse of a goddamn child.

I release her and drop to my knees. I'm trapped in my trauma, gasping for air as I'm shoved into some dark place I never wanted to be. I see and feel the abuse as if it's happening right now. Warm hands wrap around me, and

I'm too frozen in place to stop them. People who were supposed to care for me. People who were supposed to protect me. They did neither.

Aurora drops to her knees beside me, and her voice penetrates the memories. "Kane, I'm here. I'm here with you and you're going to be okay."

Her voice lacks its usual snark with an edge of mega bitch, and I allow myself to feel the comfort in her words. Her arms wrap around me, and she holds me until the visions recede into my mind and my breathing steadies.

She pulls my head against her chest. After everything I've done to her, after all the hell and torment I've put her through, she's by my side, offering her strength to me. "Not every touch is a bad touch anymore, Kane. You're past that. You're safe now."

You're. Safe. Now.

I latch onto those words as they repeat in my mind. I haven't felt safe in a long time. I've been a victim of my trauma all my life, including this very moment.

Tobin showed me these things to stop me from hurting Aurora. He's supposed to protect *me,* not *her*. But maybe, in some fucked up way, he's protecting me too. Losing Aurora would hurt more than I care to admit. He also recognizes more than I give him credit for. He's forcing me to confront my memories with someone who is willing to comfort me and help me deal with the fallout. I've never accepted comfort. Not once. But her warmth soothes me in ways I never knew were possible.

My vision becomes my own again, and I see her messy auburn hair and bright eyes full of concern. If I were her, I would have taken this freakout as yet another opportunity to run. But here she is, sitting in front of me as she tries to talk me off a ledge.

"Told you I could break through to you," she says with a smirk and a light laugh.

Jesus, this girl doesn't quit trying to irritate me. But a strained laugh comes from my chest. A chest that is still caught in a stranglehold of emotions.

Aurora leans closer, and my body tenses. She brings her hand up to my neck and draws my face toward hers. So much of what's inside me wants to push her away, to hurt her for wanting to get close to me, but some new feeling urges me to let this happen.

Her lips are so near mine now, and as her eyes close and her lips form a perfect pout, I pray to the devil that my body knows what to do with her. Then she closes that last half inch, and her warm lips are on me.

My brain is silenced the moment her lips touch mine. The memories and terror recede to their box as I focus on her scent and how she tastes. She smells like sweat and fear, a scent I usually kill for, but that homicidal rage is nowhere inside me now. Or if it is, it's buried beneath a concrete slab of need. I spread my lips and for the first time in my life, I kiss the girl.

I push her down on her back and kiss her again. She whimpers as she tugs down her pants and throws them to the side. I can only hope she remembers that I'm not Jax or Tobin. I'm surprised I'm even still hard as her hands reach for the front of my jeans and work them down. She pulls out my cock, her warm touch making me groan. I thrust my hips forward into her hand, just wanting to feel more of her. The motion feels so immature, but these feelings, these actions, are so new to me.

I sit up on my knees and spread her legs. The pussy I hated to look at looks different when I have the chance to slip inside it. It's not just something Tobin and Jax get to play with now. At this moment, it's mine.

I draw back my hips. My cock slides along the length of her slit before I thrust forward and push inside her. It's fucking heaven. She's so warm and wet. I can see why Jax and Tobin are so obsessed with her. Something so incredible should be illegal.

Considering my inexperience, I expect to move slowly and be gentle, but my body drives me to fuck her harder. I push deeper, and the soft moan that leaves her lips lets me know this is what she needs too.

"Call me daddy, dropout. Tell me how you like my cock."

"I love your cock, daddy," she pants. This time it's not snarky like at the diner or in the grave. She's saying it with pleasure woven into the word. Pleasure she's getting from me, a man who's been incapable of offering anything but pain.

With a timid hand, I raise her shirt and look at her breasts. As lust rushes over me in a wave, I'm amazed to find no anger in these waters. Only desire. My hands move toward her nipples, and I pinch and twist as she writhes beneath me.

She feels so amazing, and I want to experience her from every angle. Like a man in a desert, I want to drown myself in the oasis that is uniquely hers. I flip her onto her hands and knees, then slip inside her again with an unstifled groan. She feels even better from behind.

My hands race over her ass, squeezing the flesh as it bounces against me. I pound her pussy, my hips ricocheting off her full ass, and she whimpers from the unbridled ferocity unleashed with every thrust. Decades of pent-up frustration push inside her as I grip her hips to keep her from sliding away from me.

My tattoo rushes in and out of her as I fuck her. Keeping her nestled against me as I rail her, I bottom out inside her and force that fraction of length further until she screams. It isn't a plea for me to stop. No. She wants me to keep going.

"Come inside me, daddy!" she screams, and I love every word that leaves her lips. I love that she senses me getting close before I even notice it. A subtle change in my thrusts, I guess.

My hips stall and stutter against her ass as I fill her. I release a feral groan I don't recognize as I unleash myself inside her. It's like nothing I've ever felt.

I drop beside her and roll onto my back. Once our breathing steadies, I turn to her and look at someone I have come to care so deeply for. "It's time to get you home, dropout," I say. "Like the good little whore you are, I want you to keep my come between your legs. Can you do that?"

She leans over and kisses my forehead. "Anything for you, daddy."

I understand why Jax and Tobin want to keep her. She connected with them on multiple levels, and now she's connected with me.

And now I have to let her go.

Chapter Thirty-Three

Aurora

I bury my face in Pup's coat as I hold her. She jumped into my arms the moment we settled in the front of the truck. How she knew I'd been a day away from never being seen or heard from again is beyond me. I breathe in her scent—the outdoors with a hint of diesel.

I still don't like that Kane initially planned to sell me to those assholes, but I kind of love him for saving me and I'm thankful to be back in the truck. These are two things I never thought I'd say.

My mind still reels when I think of all that's happened in the last few hours. I got through to him. And he fucked me. He has sex like a convoluted mix of Tobin and Jax. Part rough, raw need and part passion and unquenched desire.

Kane turns onto another on-ramp, and we're heading northeast again. He's really taking me home. I have mixed feelings about this turn of events. Going home means confronting my parents with the truth, and I don't know how they'll react. Can they accept that I dropped out of college and have no desire to return? Probably not. Even if I explain the circumstances that led me to this decision, they'll turn it around on me.

But I can't stay with Kane.

I've broken through to him, but he and I both know this isn't a safe situation. He's shed some of those walls for me, but what waits behind the rest of the dilapidated exterior is what I need to fear. He's still a serial killer. A deranged man. A psychopath.

This is the textbook definition of being stuck between a rock and a hard place, but I guess the decision is out of my hands. If Kane wants to take me home, I just need to accept that this is probably his way of ensuring my safety, even though it will break my heart.

I shift in my seat. I'm sick of the silence because it only forces me to overthink, so I clear my throat. "Am I the first person you've been with since . . . ?"

"Yes. You broke through to the big, bad serial killer. Can we let it go now? I think I'm all talked out."

I smirk at him, remove Pup from my lap, and unbuckle my seatbelt. If he doesn't want to talk, that's okay by me, but I need to do something to keep my mind from spinning in circles. I drop to my knees beside him as my hand goes for his lap. His body tenses, and my breath hitches as I prepare for him to lose his shit.

"What are you doing?" he says with a tight jaw.

"I want to blow down the last of the walls surrounding the big, bad wolf," I say with a laugh. "Might as well say a proper goodbye. This is a safe space, remember?"

His muscles relax, and he licks his lips. "Get to it then, dropout."

I unbuckle and unzip his jeans. He tilts his pelvis to give me more access as I pull his cock from the fabric. I stare at the tattoo along the length of his dick and run my fingers over the flesh-warmed piercing. It's so familiar yet foreign. I've been with all three of them now, and each experience has been so different.

He *is* different.

I put my mouth on him, and he groans, the low tenor traveling to the growing heat between my legs. The metal grazes my tongue as his hand weaves through my hair, massaging my scalp before he grips the strands and impales my throat. The sheer force brings my nose against his skin. I gag, and tears well in the corners of my eyes.

This would be the point when Tobin revels in my tears or Jax apologizes for being too rough, but Kane does neither. He just tightens his grip on my head and continues using my face like an inanimate object, and fuck if that doesn't turn me on.

"You're too young and pretty to be choking on daddy's cock," he says, balling my hair in his big hand.

Control and power drip from his words. They bleed into me from the force behind his grasp as he selfishly uses my throat. He goes harder and faster, using my hair as a lead as he drives. There's no inhibition as he bucks his hips and fucks my mouth almost to the point where I need to tap out. But I'm not a quitter anymore. Tears flow down my cheeks as I fight back gags and take him the way he wants. The way he clearly needs.

"Once I come down your throat, I'm bringing you home, dropout. You'll be the only woman to leave me alive." He pulls me off his dick. "Do you understand how difficult this is for me?"

"Yes, daddy," I whimper as he cranes my neck. I wipe the drool from my chin.

He impales me on his cock again and fucks my mouth

until warm, salty come explodes down my throat. With a gravelly groan, he thrusts his hips upward and makes me take every single centimeter before he pulls out of my mouth. I swallow every drop of him.

I sit in my seat again and look out the window. Questions begin filling my mind almost immediately. Why is this difficult for him? Is it because he's grown attached to me? Or does he simply regret leaving me alive? Maybe if I knew the answers, it would change my mind. Maybe I wouldn't want to go home if he gave me a reason to stay or showed me some sign of his feelings.

But he won't. This isn't his way, and I have to accept that. Loving these three men will have to be done from a distance, and for the safety of my body and mind, I need to go home. I may be the prey who wormed her way into his blackened heart, but he's still a predator.

Chapter Thirty-Four

Jax

The truck is parked at a rest area when I shift into control. I guess Kane needed a break. I turn and look at the closed curtain separating the sleeping area from the rest of the truck. She must be asleep back there. At least, I *hope* she's asleep back there.

I go to stand, and a small note falls off of my leg. As I sit back and read the words, I can only stare in disbelief.

I SLEPT WITH AURORA. TAKE HER BACK TO NY.
KANE

Excuse me, what? There's no way. We've known Kane our whole lives, and that's just not possible. I look at the curtain again. Aurora is special, but I guess Tobin and I didn't realize just *how* special she could be.

Shifting in my seat, my gaze shifts to a pile of bloody clothes crammed inside a garbage bag. My heart stops functioning. Did Kane finally kill her?

"What the hell happened?" I whisper.

"So much," Aurora says, and I jump from my skin at the unexpected sound of her voice. The curtain rattles along the track as she pulls it open, and her big green eyes stare at me. I've never been so glad to see someone.

"Did he sell you?"

Her shoulders rise and fall in a noncommittal shrug. "Yes and no. He tried to call off the deal with those Russian guys, but they tracked his truck and kidnapped me. Kane saved me from them and . . ." She motions toward the bag of bloody clothes.

"How is this possible?"

A vortex of confusion, joy, and sadness overcomes me. I don't understand how she broke through to Kane, but I'm glad she did. I'm also sad that we have to let her go, even though it's probably for the best.

I move toward her and pull her into me. I've never been so happy to see someone, but getting to hold her now doesn't change the fact that Kane has made another decision that I can't do anything about. One that I'm even more surprised about. He's never let anyone go.

"Jax, he's letting me go home," she says, her eyes rising to meet mine.

"I know, sweet girl," I whisper, even though I hate it. But I'd rather she goes home alive than be killed here. She's too good for an unmarked grave beside the interstate. "I'm going to miss you."

She grabs my shirt and pulls me into her for a kiss. "I'll miss you too, Jax. Especially you. I'm just happy that I have a chance to say goodbye."

Tears gloss her eyes, but they disappear when she blinks.

Our last moments shouldn't be colored in a depressing

shade of blue, so I enfold her in my arms and carry her to the bed. If this is the last time I'll see her, I have to make it count. There isn't enough time to tell her all the ways I love her, so I'll just have to show her.

I grip the hem of her shirt and raise it over her head. The smile on her face tells me she's more than happy with this sort of goodbye, so I lower her pants next. I trail kisses down her stomach, losing myself to her soft curves. Her scent. Her everything. She is perfection.

She leans back on her elbows and spreads her thighs for me, and the sight of her pussy makes my mouth water. Not wanting to waste a drop of the wetness glistening on her skin, I bury my face in her heat.

Aurora lets out a soft moan as I grab her hips and tilt her pelvis to devour her further. I eat her like it's the last time I'll have my mouth on such a delicacy. Because it probably is. Her fingertips rake against my scalp as I taste her in broad strokes. My lips spread around her swollen clit, and she squirms as I lash the most sensitive part of her with my tongue.

Her screams rip through the truck and her fingertips clench my hair in an iron grip as waves of pleasure course through her. The waves crash closer together with each gentle nibble, suck, and lick.

Something knocks behind my eyes, and I can only assume it's Tobin. He's trying to come out. He wants what I'm getting, but this moment is mine. I close my eyes, blocking out the beautiful vision in front of me. He and Kane are stronger than I am, but I've never wanted anything more than this. I fight to stay here and let her come all over my face.

Aurora. Is. Mine.

Her growing wetness soaks my chin. She's so close, but

she needs more. I release her hip and push two fingers inside her. I groan, imagining that her tightening walls are around my cock.

"Jax," she pants, her chest heaving. Her beautiful tits rise and fall with every breath. I can almost feel her intense pleasure as she pulses against my tongue. Faster. Harder.

"Come for me, sweet girl," I say. "Come on my face."

Her thighs tremble beside my head. One hand drops to my shoulder and squeezes my shirt for dear life. Her back arches, and trembles wreck her body as my fingers piston in time with my tongue flicking against her sensitive clit.

"I'm coming!" she screams, and I know. Anyone within a mile would know because they'd hear those cries of pleasure. Melodic sounds like that only mean one thing.

I ride out every shudder of her orgasm until she softly jerks with every full lick of my tongue. When I'm sure she's finished, I lean over her and press my lips to hers, spreading all her pleasure onto her chin. She kisses me back, and it's something I'll never experience again. My desire and need are tethered to her for eternity.

"Good girl, coming so hard on my face. You soaked my chin."

I pull away and wipe her come from my chin with the back of my hand, and then I slide the fingers that were in her pussy into her mouth. She licks them clean without hesitation.

God, I'll miss her.

She has brought out the best parts of all of us. What will we become once she's gone?

Chapter Thirty-Five

Aurora

We've been on the road for what feels like forever. Kane is trying to get me home as soon as possible, probably so that he doesn't change his mind. I'm still lying in bed after my time with Jax, listening to the road noise and trying my best to fall asleep. My mind wanders down well-worn paths, but I'm no closer to the answers.

For starters, what will I say to my parents when I return home after being radio silent for so long? I've gotten close to home before and never actually made it, and it's time to admit that I've been avoiding this reunion. But Kane is encouraging me to go through with it, so I'll try.

It's not like I have another option. If I can't be with Kane, Jax, and Tobin, I can't be with anyone. Turning back to my former sex work would feel like cheating. Even if they can't keep me, I'll always keep a piece of them tucked inside my heart.

The truck pulls into a parking lot, and I turn over and

pretend to be asleep. I'm trying so hard to keep my distance now. Saying goodbye to Kane and Jax was already painful enough. If I get closer to any of them, it will be that much harder to leave.

The curtain slides across the track, and a heavy exhale precedes heavy boot steps. The mattress sinks as he sits on the edge of the bed, pushing my back against his. I try not to think about the warmth and comfort this unintentional touch provides because if I do, I'll probably cry. He pulls off each boot, and they thud against the floor as he tosses them down. The blanket draws back, and he gets into bed.

I don't even know who's presenting right now. I can tell by their facial expressions, voice, and sometimes the way they touch me, but I'm staring at the metal wall beside my head, he's silent, and he hasn't reached for me, which makes me think it might be Kane. He isn't the type to cuddle, even after our breakthrough. I wish it was something I could learn to accept, but I haven't been afforded the time.

His warmth is just what I need to fall asleep, and I'm finally dozing off when a heavy arm drapes over me. His hand glides along my hip, and the touch is too gentle to be anyone but my sweet Jax. I back into him, and his heat engulfs me.

"Jax?" I whisper.

"Not Jax, eighty," Tobin says, his warm tenor dripping from each word. "I'm glad to see you."

I roll toward him, a sad smile on my face because this means it's his turn to say goodbye. "Told you I could get through to him," I say.

"I don't know how."

"Don't pretend you didn't unleash those memories. You knew I'd comfort him."

A sinner's smirk slides across his face. "I couldn't let him do what he was about to do."

He wraps his arm around me and pulls me against his chest. I thought he only viewed me as a nice fuck, but he's actually cuddling me. Being tender. I guess this goodbye is affecting him more than I realized.

Tobin places his fingers beneath my chin and tips my face toward his. I swallow before meeting him the rest of the way and taking his mouth. They each give me something I need, and right now, I need Tobin. He's so tactile, using pleasure and pain as instruments for ultimate fulfillment. He's precisely what I need to forget about the fact that I have to go home.

Without them.

"You're really leaving us, eighty?" he whispers against my lips.

"I think this is what Kane wants."

Tobin nods. "It's probably for the best. Kane isn't always in control, even when he is in control. Even if it isn't for the best for all of us, you'll be better off."

Will I be better off? Kane and Tobin worked hard to break me, emotionally and sexually. They shaped me until I was a puzzle piece forced into place in their world. And now? Now I'm being tossed back home because I fit too well. I can handle their fucked-up, confusing puzzle, and they don't know what to do with that.

"I don't think he would hurt me," I say.

"You're so fucking hurtable. Everything about you makes me want to hurt you. But the difference is, to me, you're also so fuckable. I want to please you after I cause you pain. Kane isn't like that."

"I think Kane likes fucking me now," I say.

"You fucked him?"

I nod.

"Tell me about it, eighty. How'd you fuck Kane?"

Tobin rolls me onto my belly and gets above me. His body presses me into the mattress as his hand weaves through my hair and cranes my neck.

"He fucked me after killing the men who took me," I say, straining to get the words out beneath his weight.

Tobin leans off me just enough to rip down my pants, but he keeps my legs pinned together beneath him. He brings a hand to his mouth and spits before wiping it between my legs.

"Did he make you call him daddy?" The warmth of his cock fills the void between my thighs as he waits for me to answer.

"Yes," I whimper. "And then I sucked his dick while he was driving."

He thrusts forward, and I scream out from the sudden intrusion. He feels even bigger like this, like he's impaling me.

"Did his cock make you cry when he forced it down your throat?" He punctuates each word with a hard, driven thrust.

"Yes," I say, fighting back the tremble in my voice.

He keeps ramming into me, each pleasurable jolt intensified by the presence of pain. If he wasn't holding my legs together, I would probably rip in two from the force of his jealousy. The ferocity in his driven motions forces tears past the creases of my lids.

"That's a good girl. Cry for me. I want your eyes as wet as your cunt."

Then his tattooed hand wraps around my throat and squeezes. There's no warning with Tobin. He just cuts off my breath like I never deserved to have any in the first place.

"You're such a good girl for us, eighty. Such a well-trained little slut. Shame to let you go. I'll miss this cunt." He pushes into me again, then leans over until his warm breath whispers over the shell of my ear. "I'll miss *you*."

My heart soars when he says those words. He reinforces the hope that I was more to him than just a good lay. I mean something to a man who values so little.

"We're almost in New York now," he says as he leans back and fucks me hard again. "I want you to go back to your parents with my come between your pretty thighs."

He flips me over, goes to the galley, and comes back with a wooden spoon. The feral glint in his eyes tells me exactly what he plans to do. As he slides inside me again, he brushes the head of the spoon along my slit before slapping it against my sensitive flesh.

I let out a whimper and he does it again, this time spreading my lips so the spoon can come in contact with my clit. Pain and pleasure ricochet through me, and I clench around him as a scream breaks from my throat.

"You like that, eighty? You like the pain?" He does it again as I nod, and another bolt shoots through me. If he keeps this up, I'm going to come.

Sensing this, he tosses the spoon away and flips me onto my stomach again. He wants to tease me.

His hand snakes around my throat, and he cuts off my breath again as the rocking motion of his thrusts grinds my pussy against the mattress. I grip the sheets as he fucks me in the selfish way I've grown to expect with him. With my breath gone and my chest heaving for air, I'm teetering over the edge of an orgasm.

I want him to remember me the way I'll remember him.

I want to squeeze his shaft with my pussy as he explodes inside me. I need to give him the best orgasm he's ever had.

I can't scream out, but the pleasure slams into me as stars dance in front of my eyes. My muscles tighten and spasm as I orgasm without my most basic necessity. Oxygen. He releases my neck, and I inhale a sharp breath as he comes with a force I can feel throughout my body. The ripple effect of his pleasure shakes me to my core. With a loud, unrestrained groan, his hand leaves my hair to slam into the metal wall, a byproduct of the intense orgasm I hoped to give him.

Tobin pulls out of me, turns me onto my back, and presses his mouth to mine. His tongue rips through my lips as he kisses me with a passion I've never seen from him.

He pulls back and brushes my hair away from my face. "You have my heart, eighty. I won't be out for a while, so consider this my goodbye." He leans down and kisses me again.

I never thought I'd see this side of Tobin. He's still so gruff, but I see the sweetness beneath the rough exterior. And it's too much. I don't want to say goodbye. To any of them.

Tears slip down my cheeks, and I lift my hand to wipe them away. He stops me and brings his tongue to my cheek, licking a long line up my skin, cleaning the tears from my face.

"Let me keep those inside me. As a part of me." His lips draw into a smirk. "You know I like it when you cry for me."

Chapter Thirty-Six

Jax

There's no way Kane could meet her parents without making everyone extremely uncomfortable, so I was thrust into the driver's seat as we neared her family's home. It would sound as if she'd been kidnapped if he'd been the one to explain this situation. Kane is so bad at being around other humans.

I pick up the note Kane left on the dashboard and turn it over in my hands. The paper has been folded into a small square. I haven't read it yet. I plan to wait until I'm around Aurora. Then I'll say goodbye to her for the last time.

My heart aches when I glance at her. She's wearing a clean shirt and a new pair of jeans. Kane took her to a store and bought her an outfit because she couldn't go home in what she was wearing when we found her. I offered to stop to let her shower, but she said she made a promise to Tobin and couldn't. I can only imagine.

"Do we have a story?" she asks as she fidgets in the passenger seat. Pup sleeps on her lap. It's her usual spot now, and I'm worried the poor dog may take the loss just as hard as we will.

"You should probably start by telling your parents you dropped out of college."

Her lips tighten. "I guess I have to."

"It won't hurt to dilute the truth a little, though. Just say you've been traveling across the country. We picked you up and brought you back home." I smile at her. "Maybe omit the parts about being a sex worker."

She hits my arm and we both laugh. Damn it, I'm going to miss her.

She gives me directions to her house when we're nearly there. It's the only house on the road, with a thruway running behind it. I can't see it, but I know it's there. I ease the truck up the long driveway, get out of the driver's seat, and go around to open the door for Aurora. She clutches Pup to her chest, giving her a long stroke and a kiss on the top of her head.

"No more running off, Pup," she whispers. "I won't be there to save you next time." She swipes the tears from her eyes, places Pup on the floor, and reaches for my hand.

I help her down. Before we even make it to the front steps, the door swings open, showcasing the confused expressions of her parents.

"Jesus Christ, Aurora! We've been trying to get in touch with you for so long!" Her mother's confused anger turns to happiness as she pulls her daughter into her. "Where have you been?"

"Everywhere," Aurora says. Her voice is flat, completely devoid of the life, snark, and lilt I've heard since she's been with us.

Her short-and-stout father peers behind me, his gaze

bolting to my truck after gripping Aurora's shoulder. "What a beauty you got."

"You drove trucks too, right?"

"I was regional before I became local. Then I hung up the keys to be with my wife," he says, but there's an intense longing in his eyes as he stares at my truck. Once a trucker, always a trucker. "But my truck never looked like that!"

I draw his attention back to me by clearing my throat. "Well, I'd best get going."

"Nonsense!" her mother says. "Come in and have some dinner!"

Aurora and I look at each other. Yeah, if Kane was here, he'd keel over from the mention of dinner with Aurora's parents. Lucky for him, I'm always down to socialize. I nod, and her parents welcome me inside.

Family pictures adorn every surface of the quaint home. A lot of the pictures are missing the father. Most show a mother alongside her daughter, looking like a piece of their life is missing. He must have been gone a lot. If I had a family, I'm not sure I'd pick this business. The money is good, sure, and If you don't like your family and want to be away from them as much as possible, this job is great. But if you want to spend time with someone you like, it's hard.

Unless you can bring them across state lines like we did with Aurora.

That creates its own problems, though, and I don't just mean the risk Kane poses to her safety. Because three of us live in the same body, I'd never get enough time with her. I'd be away, like a trucker, no matter how close I am.

Her mother leads us into the kitchen, and the scent of home-cooked soup fills the room.

"You're lucky your mother makes enough of her famous chicken noodle soup to feed the whole city," her father says before sitting down at the table. Her mother exits the kitchen, and he turns to Aurora as she and I take a seat. "So you've been riding with this guy?"

"Jax," I say, introducing myself as I hold out my hand.

He takes it and gives it a shake. "Jax, huh?" He turns to Aurora again. "You've been traveling all over with him after college?"

Aurora swallows, and I reach beneath the table to grip her leg and provide the reassurance she needs. She can do this. She can do fucking anything.

"Dad, I have to tell you something."

"If you're pregnant, don't tell me. I don't think my old ticker can handle it," he says, giving me a death glare.

"You're *pregnant*?" Her mom comes around the corner, having only heard the worst part of that conversation.

I shake my head, and Aurora sighs.

"I'm not pregnant, Jesus Christ," she says. "Just let me get this out, please."

Her mom sits down in the chair beside her father.

"Mom, Dad . . . I dropped out of college."

I watch as her parents' lips draw into the tightest frowns I've ever seen. Judging by their sour expressions, maybe unplanned pregnancy would have been the better story.

"What the fuck do you mean you dropped out of school?" her father shouts. His face changes shades until finally settling on red. No wonder she didn't want to tell them. It isn't going great.

I'm very good at peopling, but I'm not as good with conflict. Kane would be better for this moment, but I'm stuck here.

"School isn't for everyone," I say in a weak attempt to calm him down, but it just angers him further.

He turns his glazed gaze to me. "I'd advise you to shut your mouth, son. This is a family matter."

I lean back and shut my mouth. That's when I feel Kane knocking. Maybe he can sense my rising heart rate. My panic. I'm usually cool as a cucumber, but I don't love this situation.

"Don't talk to him like that, Dad!" Aurora snaps. "I chose to leave school, and he had nothing to do with it. I didn't meet him until I'd started traveling."

Her father stands up and walks around the table, heading straight for Aurora. I stand and get between them. As much as I hate conflict, no one will put their hands on her. Even if we can't keep her, she will always be ours.

"Hey, why don't we all relax and have some dinner," her mother says.

Her father takes a step back and throws his hands up. "Fine, but this discussion isn't over."

I'm sure she'll get an earful when I'm gone, but I'm glad I could be a buffer for now—even if it's making me anxious as hell. I'd deal with anything for Aurora.

I sit at the table as her mother serves dinner with a sour scowl. I've hardly tasted the soup when her father turns to me. Though he's looking right into my eyes, his words are aimed squarely at Aurora. "Why don't you say goodbye to your friend now?"

I nod and stand up, pushing the chair beneath the table. "I think that's best. Let's get your stuff out of the truck."

I motion Aurora toward the front door and bring her outside. She walks to the truck and climbs up to grab her backpack from between the seats. When she has both feet on the ground again, she stares at the paper I've pulled from my pocket.

I pull her into me. "First, I want to say goodbye as me.

As Jax." The truck shields this moment from prying eyes, so I lean down and kiss her. I hold her, squeezing her until a laugh leaves her lips. That sweet sound is something I want to imprint on my memory. "Goodbye, sweet girl. I love you."

Her lower lip begins to quiver, and I push on before she can start crying. I don't know if I can keep going if I see her tears.

"And now, this is from Kane." I clear my throat and lower my voice to bring forth Kane's tenor the best I can. Then I unfold the paper and begin to read. "Kane here. I can't be there to see you off, so this is the best I can do. I'm not sorry for the things I did to break you when all it did was make you stronger. I'm not sorry for selling you to The Nameless because it made me realize that I couldn't let you go. I *am* sorry for having to let you go now. I can't keep you safe because no one is safe from me and the shit decisions I make. I want you to be happy, no matter how unhappy that makes me. Don't argue about it, because I won't change my mind. You survived the I-90 Killer, and as soon as you hear that name, I know you'll recognize who I am. You survived me and . . . won me over. Just like you wanted. This is goodbye, but that's a good thing for you, even if it doesn't feel like it right now. So . . . goodbye, dropout."

When I lower the letter, my heart breaks into a thousand pieces. She's crying, and it's the sort of sobbing I can't soothe away. Our time is up.

"I love you too, Jax. You cared for me when no one else did." She wipes her face, removing the proof of her pain. "Can I keep that?"

It literally admits who Kane is. As Kane's protector, everything inside me says no. But as Aurora's friend, I'm compelled to hand it over to her.

She takes it and puts it into her pocket, then pulls me

into her. "Goodbye, Jax." She places a kiss on my right cheek. "Goodbye, Tobin." Her lips press against my left cheek, accompanied by a slight nibble. Then she kisses my lips and leans closer to my ear. "And you too, Daddy Kane. Goodbye."

Chapter Thirty-Seven

Aurora

I've made it forty-eight hours, but I can't stop feeling like I'm crawling out of my skin. My parents haven't even spoken to me. Instead of sitting down and having a discussion, they mope around the house with scowls on their faces. I left school, and they can't get past that. They probably wish I'd been missing after all. Dead somewhere. At least I wouldn't be their college fucking dropout.

I walk into the living room. Based on the bottles at his feet, my father is already seven beers deep. His glassy eyes never leave the television. My mom's nowhere to be found. The whole house is silent except for the low sounds coming from the TV.

"Well, if it isn't my disappointment," he says with a cheeriness that grates against my nerves. "Come sit down beside your dear old dad."

I hesitate, but he slaps the cushion beside him. I knock into a bottle as I walk over and sit down. The glass hits the hardwood and rolls.

"You know, I left my job, a job I *loved*, to be more of a parent to you." His voice slurs with each word, and the fetid scent of gut-fermented alcohol rolls toward me. "I did that, and then you go and shit on me by dropping out of college."

"Dad, I left because . . ." I can't seem to form the words to tell him what happened to me. He's my father, for fuck's sake. Even if the awkward factor was removed, he'd probably only victim-blame anyway.

His fiery eyes leave the TV and finally land on me. He clambers off the couch and stands over me. "There is no reason you can possibly conjure up that would make up for me leaving my job and turning in life insurance policies to pay for your fucking schooling. Inconsiderate bitch."

He draws back his hand and slaps me across the face. Aside from blinking to clear the sting in my eyes, I don't react. I learned my stoicism at an early age.

Then his words finally reach my ears, and I have to stuff down the anger. I was never the one who wanted him to give up his job, and I sure as shit didn't ask him to fund my schooling. That was all my mother. I'm not sure why she wanted him home to begin with. His temper has always been terrible.

A burning pain blazes beneath my right eye, and I can already sense the bruise forming beneath my skin. This isn't the first mark he's left on me, and it won't be the last if I stay here.

I stand and push past him. He stumbles backward, then tries to follow me, but I'm already in my bedroom. I lock the door and go to the desk beside my bed.

When I was twelve, my dad bought a CB radio and set it up in my room. He taught me how to use it, but I never took much interest in it. Now, I couldn't be more grateful for it.

I turn it on, and a crackle of static punches through the speakers. My fingers shake as I turn to the same frequency Kane used in his truck. Then I grab the microphone and squeeze. The silence tells me I can speak and possibly be heard.

"Three Amigos, are you out there?" I release the button and the static continues again. No one answers. "Three Amigos, this is Dropout. Can you hear me?"

I try for so long I sound desperate. It's been two days, so he's probably too far gone to hear me now. He'd have to be nearby, but he's probably long gone.

"Three Amigos," I say once more. When no one answers, I squeeze the mic one last time. "I'll try again tomorrow."

I UNLOCK my bedroom door and head for the bathroom in the morning. I glance at my face in the mirror and quickly look away. Just like I thought, a nice shiner mars my cheek. It's purple and pink, nice and fresh. Can't wait to explain that to my mother.

Who am I kidding? She'll play dumb when she sees it. She's completely blind to bruises that come from my father's hands.

I thought things would have changed since I've been gone. The last time I spoke to my mother, she said my father had stopped drinking and was a "new man," so either my mother lied or my college status derailed his sobriety that much. Either way, I shouldn't have come home. Kane brought me here because he thought I'd be safe. I'm no safer here than I was in Kane's truck, but at least I had some happiness with them.

Even with Kane.

I go into the kitchen for breakfast. My mother notices my face and gasps, but she doesn't respond to it directly. Instead, she turns back to the vegetables on the cutting board and starts dicing them. I'm so glad to know the breakfast omelet is more important than my well-being.

"I really wish you would have stayed in school," she finally says.

"Well, I didn't, and *I* wish you guys would accept that."

"Your father won't."

"Then what am I doing here?"

"I don't know." She lowers the knife, and her shoulders drop. "I thought it would be different."

"Did you think I'd come home and be super successful, and then you'd love me?"

She turns to face me. "We do love you. Even if you aren't successful."

"Jesus Christ. Forget breakfast. I'm not hungry."

I go back to the bedroom, lock my door, and flip on the radio. Idle chatter breaks through the static, something about nearby construction, but I don't hear any recognizable call signs.

I click the button and speak over the radio. "Three Amigos, this is Dropout. Come in."

"You sound pretty. How old are you, Dropout?" someone says.

"I'm looking for Three Amigos. If you aren't him, fuck off," I say.

"Ooh wee, you got a mouth on you."

"Dropout, this is Three Amigos, and if Jangles doesn't

get off this fucking station, I'll cut his balls off the next time I see him."

The other man disappears, though I'm unsure if he's still listening. Either way, I don't care. The prospect of talking to Kane warms me. I know it's him because I recognize that low, annoyed southern twang.

"Three Amigos, I'm having a bad time here. Over." I release the button and rest the mic on my lap.

"Copy that." His rich voice blares from the speakers, and I lower the volume to keep my parents from hearing. I'm too old for this, but I can't let my father take away my one tie to Kane and the boys. "Having trouble adjusting to life, Dropout? I know damn well you can adjust to just about anything."

"No. It's not that. I just want to come home. Over."

"You are home."

"No, this isn't my home anymore. That truck is my home. *You* are my home."

After a long pause, he responds. "Are you out of your mind? This isn't the place for you."

I sigh and click the button again, but my voice breaks before I can say anything else. My parents don't want me, and it's clear he doesn't want me either.

I raise the mic again. "You know what? This was stupid. Roger that. Dropout, over and out."

I'm literally just spewing radio lingo at this point. I throw the microphone onto the desk and climb into bed. My heart aches for them, but I won't beg him. He should know that by now.

I start to doze off as the hours pass by, but I'm startled awake by the sound of the radio.

"Dropout, this is Three Amigos. You there?"

I don't reach for the microphone because I'm petty and still irritated. I slam a pillow over my head.

"I know you're there," Kane says, low and almost sweet. "I'm still here." Which means he pulled over somewhere to stay within radius.

I grab the microphone. "Why are you still here?"

"Because you don't ask for help unless you need it. Shit, even if you need it, you're not likely to ask."

Fair.

"I don't want help," I say. "I just want you."

"Beg for me, Dropout."

"Wh-what? I'm not doing that over the radio."

"Give the other truckers a show, and I'll come pick you up."

Even when he's not here, he wants to degrade me. Am I sure I want to go back to this guy?

My internal thoughts respond with an instantaneous *yes*.

I turn over and bring the microphone close to my mouth. "Please, daddy. I need you," I moan. "I'll do *any*thing if you come get me. Anything. Please."

"Play with yourself," he commands.

Are we really doing this over public radio? Where any trucker in radius can hear me? He's making me feel like a CB whore—the kind you pick up on this damn thing—and I think that's what he wants me to feel like. Typical Kane.

I drop my hand between my legs, click the button, and rub myself as I moan and plead over the radio for him.

"That moaning won't cut it, Dropout. Tell me what you're doing to yourself."

My cheeks flame hot. Considering my profession was sex work for a while, this shouldn't embarrass me like it does, but my jobs were always private. But this? I'm servicing an entire fleet at once.

But if I want Kane, if I want Jax and Tobin, I have to play along.

I clear my throat and press the button. "I'm sliding my fingers through my slit. I'm so wet for you, daddy."

When my finger slips off the button, the excited chatter of other men fills the silence, their desperation dripping from their thirsty words. But I can't stop or Kane won't come get me.

"I'm imagining your cock stretching me so fucking good. Don't you want to come pick me up so you can feel me tightening around you?"

I let go of the button and hope he'll say yes, that I can stop. Instead, a stranger's voice comes through. "Shit, if he won't come pick you up, I sure as fuck will."

My eyes roll. After experiencing what Kane and his alters have to offer, nothing else could ever compare. "No thanks," I say into the mic. "But it sure would be a shame to let all this wetness go to waste, wouldn't it, Three Amigos?"

Keeping the button depressed, I bring my fingers to my lips and suck them.

"I taste so good, daddy. Don't you want to taste?" I pause. "Or would you rather choke me with your cock?"

I release the button and close my eyes as static pours from the speakers. Then I smile when his voice comes over the radio.

"I'm outside your house, Dropout. Get your ass out here."

Chapter Thirty-Eight

Kane

I'm so stupid for driving back here for her, but how could I resist her desperation over the radio? I tried for as long as I could. Instead of going back on route, I hung around because I couldn't stop thinking about her. The truck is really fucking lonely without her, and Pup is driving me batshit with all the whining and pacing.

Aurora knows who I am now. She knows the true me. The I-90 Killer. A man who has been thought to be responsible for so many deaths. A man every police agency desperately wants to catch. She's in love with a murderer. If she wants to come with me, then she's accepted the risk of being with me.

With us.

I sit and wait in her driveway. When the door to her house opens, yelling follows. Someone isn't happy that she plans to leave again. From the note Jax left for me, I learned they weren't happy about her coming home either.

She whips open the passenger side door and climbs into the truck. That's when I see her fucking cheek.

I grab her face and turn it so I can have a better look at the pink and purple bruising all along her face. "Who did this to you?" I ask, though I'm certain I know the answer. Her fucking father—the man standing in the doorway and staring me down. "Did he do this?"

She nods, and it's all the confirmation I need. I undo my seat belt and whip open the door.

Her hand wraps around my arm and squeezes. "Don't hurt him, Kane, please! Promise me!"

I want to do more than hurt him, but I also want to have some kind of fucked-up life with Aurora. That won't be possible if I get put away for assault. Or, in this case, what would surely be murder.

Without promising her anything, I exit the truck and walk toward the doorway. Her father tries to slam the door in my face, but I catch it with my hand, ignore the pain, and push it open.

"I won't fucking hurt you," I say as I push him against the wall. "I won't do that because she asked me not to, even though you clearly deserve it. But if I'm going to leave this house without putting you in a fucking wheelchair, you have to agree that you won't ever contact her again. Don't even try." I turn to her mother. "That goes for you too."

"You can't just take our daughter!" she shrieks. The sound makes me want to commit homicide twelve different ways. It also shows me where Aurora inherited that awful ability to make such a sound.

"I'm not taking her. She's leaving of her own free will because she's an adult. Have a terrible fucking night, you two." I slam the door behind me as I leave without saying another word. I've made my goddamn point.

It takes everything in me to leave her father alive. No one puts a hand on what belongs to me. But her desperate plea to leave him unharmed replays in my mind, and I force myself off the steps. My hands are shaking by the time I climb into the truck. Aurora looks at them to see if there's blood.

"I didn't hurt them, but we have to go before I do. Self-control is not my strong suit."

"Thank you," she whispers.

I nod at her, put the truck in reverse, and drive her far away from the home I thought she needed to be in. I was wrong, and Tobin and Jax are going to be fucking ecstatic about that. Pup is already showing her joy by licking Aurora's face and turning happy circles in her lap.

They aren't the only ones who have a reason to be happy about our turn of events, I guess. I just don't show it the same way they do. I'll never be like them, but that's why she has them. They can give her the love she needs and wants. I can give her my vulnerability. That's all she ever wanted from me anyway.

Epilogue

Aurora

Being with all three of them has been a difficult—but often pleasant—challenge. I don't know who I'll wake up beside at any given moment. I won't know until I can see their expression or hear their voice. I won't know until I hear the nickname they call me. I know by the way they touch me. Or if they even touch me at all. And I always know by the way they love me. Each one cares for me in different ways—with more or less of themselves, but always with all their heart.

Jax loves to love me. He lives to please me and make me laugh.

Tobin loves to hurt me and then make it all better with a touch that none of them can replicate, despite having the same hands.

Kane . . . To love Kane is to hate him too. He can be the most insufferable man to be around. Angry, miserable, bitter about all that life offered him. Except for me. I'm the little bit of what life offered him that wasn't shit. He hates so many things, but he lets me curl up under his arm and call him daddy as he strokes my back until he calms down.

Tobin turns over and wraps his arm around me, then pulls me against his hard body. "Morning, eighty," he says.

I didn't see Tobin for a while after I came back. He must have been upset when I left. When he finally came out, he was so surprised. Once the shock wore off, he fucked me for hours. He wouldn't get off me until he made up for every day we were apart.

"Morning," I whisper, letting his hand race over my body. His touch pulls me away from every thought until I can focus on nothing more than his fingertips on me.

Pup stretches beside me and hops to the floor. She gives herself a good shake, her collar rattling. I lean over the side of the bed and run my hand through her fur. She looks up at me with her glossy brown eyes and gives a little bark. It's her way of saying good morning.

My life is so different from what it was. I finally feel like I have a purpose that doesn't involve those three numbers. Forty-sixty-eighty. I'm free from so much more than that, though. I no longer have to worry about going home and trying to force myself into a life I don't fit into anymore.

Home is here in this truck.

Home is Kane, Tobin, and Jax.

Home is a little dog who ran away and brought four people together.

I've found something most people can only dream about. I go to sleep in one part of the country and wake up in another. I go to sleep with one man and wake up with another too. Yeah, this life is a little complicated at times.

But clearly, I like it that way.

If you enjoyed this story, check out the rest of my dark, hitchhiker romance standalones in the Ride or Die series. These can be read in any order.

Hitched: Books2read.com/Hitched
Along for the Ride: Books2read.com/MFMHitchhiker
Driving my Obsession: Books2read.com/DrivingmyObsession
Don't Stop: Books2read.com/Dont-Stop

If you need some palate cleansers after this read, check out these short, spicy reads.

Stranger Session: Books2read.com/StrangerSession
Her Fantasy: Books2read.com/HerFantasy
Last Mistake: Books2read.com/LastMistake

Connect with Lauren

Find all of my books, social media connections, and other important information at: Campsite.bio/LaurenBielAuthor or LaurenBiel.com

Join the group on Facebook to connect with other fans and to discuss the books with the author. Visit http://www.facebook.com/groups/laurenbieltraumances for more!

Lauren is now on Patreon! Get access to even more content and sneak peeks at upcoming novels. Check it out at www.patreon.com/LaurenBielAuthor to learn more!

Acknowledgments

I wouldn't be able to do this without the continued support from my readers. I am so thankful for all of you!

A special thank you to my sensitivity readers! @SL McGinnis (check out her books!), @Lyla_sky_reads, and @Ariel Zucca for making sure I didn't create any harmful stereotypes related to Dissociative Identity Disorder.

I appreciate my friend Gregory B. (love you!) and reader Savannah McCarthy (bananarae_bookish) for helping me write about trucker life.

To my VIP gals (Lori, Kimberly, Jessie, Nikita, Lexi, Grace), I love you so much!

Thank you to my husband for dealing with me every day like some kind of saint.

Thank you to my editor, Brooke, for making this book perfect.

Thank you to my valued Patrons. Your contribution helped make this book happen!

Lori R, Jessie, Michelle M, Tabitha F, Lindsey S, Erika M, Laura T, Nicole M, Nineette W, Kimberly B, BoneDaddy-

Ashe, Kimberly S, Sammi Rae, Sarah, Allison B, Andrea J, Chelle, Gabby S, Jennifer H, Jessica G, Juli D, Samantha R, Sara S,@bethbetweenthepages, Sharee S, Samantha W, Lourdes G, Kelli T, Shelby F, Lauren P, Mackenzie H, Tiannah B, Wombles, Kristiana B, Vero A, Berthie, Deani, Amanda C, Brooke O, Liza M, Ashley P, Mandy, Maddy, Cynthia B, Courtney P, Kate, Lisa A, Leslie W, Mrs Mandy, Jordyn J, DJ Krimmer, Kayla M, Marisa, Jess M, Amber, Lori, Tiffany T, Smitty, Anna S

Also by Lauren Biel

To view Lauren Biel's complete list of books, visit: https://laurenbiel.com/laurenbielbooks/

About the Author

Lauren Biel is the author of many dark romance books with several more titles in the works. When she's not working, she's writing. When she's not writing, she's spending time with her husband, her friends, or her pets. You might also find her on a horseback trail ride or sitting beside a waterfall in Upstate New York. When reading her work, expect the unexpected. To be the first to know about her upcoming titles, please visit www.LaurenBiel.com.

Made in the USA
Monee, IL
21 September 2024

66275921R00163